I flung out my arms. 'Look around you. The Bolton Canteen. The Mackenzie Allan Studio. The SuperSports Gym.'

'You've missed out the Kingston Medical Room,' said Jazz. 'And it seems like you should be heading straight there yourself.'

'They're all named after big businesses who've donated money to the school,' I swept on regardless. Honestly, if I responded to every insult hurled at me, we'd be here all day. 'What about if we could get something at Coppergate named after Mum?'

There was silence. I had been glowing with excitement but now I suddenly felt unsure of myself as still no one said anything.

'I think I just saw a pig flying across the sky,' Geena said faintly. 'For once, Amber has *actually* had a truly great idea.'

www.narinderdhami.com

superstar babes

narinder dhami

CORGI YEARLING BOOKS

SUPERSTAR BABES
A CORGI YEARLING BOOK 978 0 440 86845 3

Published in Great Britain by Corgi Yearling,
an imprint of Random House Children's Books
A Random House Group Company

This edition published 2008

1 3 5 7 9 10 8 6 4 2

Copyright © Narinder Dhami, 2008

Penguin Random House is committed to a sustainable future for
our business, our readers and our planet. This book is made from
Forest Stewardship Council® certified paper.

MIX
Paper from
responsible sources
FSC® C018179

Printed and bound in Great Britain by Clays Ltd, St Ives plc

Set in Palatino by
Falcon Oast Graphic Art Ltd.

Corgi Yearling Books are published by Random House Children's Books,
61–63 Uxbridge Road, London W5 5SA

www.**kids**at**random**house.co.uk
www.**rbooks**.co.uk

Addresses for companies within The Random House Group Limited can
be found at: www.randomhouse.co.uk/offices.htm

THE RANDOM HOUSE GROUP Limited Reg. No. 954009

A CIP catalogue record for this book is available from the British Library.

superstar babes

Chapter One

'You've got *all* my money now, Amber!' Jazz shrieked, hurling a fistful of banknotes at me. 'There are times when I really, *really* hate you!'

I smiled with quiet satisfaction and began gathering up the scattered notes. Meanwhile Jazz vented her frustration by whacking me round the head with a pillow. I yelped with surprise and grabbed a ruler off the desk next to the bed to defend myself.

'I'm only asking you to pay what you owe!' I shouted, poking her hard in the ribs. 'I can't help it if I'm financially brilliant and have a fantastic business brain!'

Jazz picked up a biro and we began to fence, lunging and parrying like Olympic champions.

'Oh, please,' said Geena, picking up the dice. 'This is meant to be a perfectly civilized game of

Monopoly. There's no need to go over the top.'

'It's not fair,' Jazz grumbled, attempting to stick the biro into my arm. 'Amber always buys expensive places like Mayfair and puts hotels on them and then it costs us hundreds of pounds.'

'Really, Jazz!' Geena said in a superior manner. 'It *is* only a game. One, two, three, four . . .' She moved her top hat around the board and her face fell. 'Oh dear.'

'Oh, look,' I pointed out. 'You've landed on my hotel in Park Lane. That's—'

'Whatever it is, I don't have enough,' Geena snapped, fanning out a paltry collection of notes.

'I told you not to buy Liverpool Street Station.' I wagged my finger at her. 'The railway stations never make much money. Well, it looks like I'm the supreme Monopoly champion. *Again*.'

Geena shot me a bitter look.

'Remember, Geena, it's only a game,' I reminded her.

Geena didn't answer. She just launched herself at me and began trying to stuff her feeble collection of banknotes down the back of my T-shirt. Very undignified behaviour for a girl of fifteen, wouldn't you say? Jazz, who's only a twelve-year-old *child*, immediately joined in. This is the problem with having sisters so close in age to me (a very mature almost-fourteen-year-old). They're *so* competitive.

'You two appear to be rather bad losers,' I spluttered, trying to fend them off.

'Ha!' Geena said savagely, pinning me down on the duvet. 'Where's your *Get out of jail free* card now, Amber?'

'*Do not pass GO*,' Jazz intoned, bouncing up and down on my legs. '*Do not collect two hundred pounds. Do not annoy your sisters or you'll end up dead.*'

Even though I was face-down on the bed with a mouthful of duvet, my mind was working overtime, as usual. This, at a rough count, was the seventeenth argument we'd had this week. Seventeen arguments about Monopoly and things which had been borrowed without permission and whose turn it was to take out the rubbish – that kind of nonsense. Fifteen of them had ended in mild violence. The other two hadn't, only because Dad had put a stop to them.

Maybe something significant was going on here.

'Stop!' I shouted through the duvet.

'That's strange,' said Geena. 'I thought I heard Amber tell us to *stop*. She said it as if we were actually going to *obey* her.'

'How ridiculous,' Jazz commented, shoving the Community Chest cards down my front, appropriately enough, along with the rest of the banknotes. 'Pass me the Monopoly board, Geena. I have plans for it.'

'No, you don't understand.' I managed to roll over, even with Geena weighing me down. 'I know why we're arguing like this.'

'So do we,' Geena replied. 'You bankrupted us with an extremely annoying and very smug smile on your face, so now we're exacting our revenge.'

'Very well put,' Jazz approved.

'I don't mean *this*.' With an effort I threw them off and jumped to my feet. Cards and notes from the Monopoly game showered down around me, falling out from under the hem of my T-shirt. 'I mean, I know why we're arguing *all* the time.'

'I thought that was normal,' Jazz said.

'Well, kind of,' I agreed. 'But it's been worse since Auntie got married and moved out, wouldn't you say?'

Auntie had moved in with us months ago and had immediately set about interfering in our lives with determination and, quite frankly, a great deal of glee. Before she arrived from India, it was just us three and Dad. Our mum died almost two years ago after she'd been ill for a while. Auntie had taken charge of everything and still liked to think she had us under her thumb, even though she'd now got married to the gorgeous Mr Arora, a teacher at our school, and moved out. Mind you, she'd only moved next door.

'I know exactly what's going on,' I said thoughtfully. 'We're arguing so much because we're *bored*. We need a new project. Something to get our teeth into.'

Geena sighed loudly. 'Amber, if this is some pathetic attempt to reason with Jazz and me before we beat you to a pulp, I can tell you that it isn't working.'

'No, it isn't.' Jazz brandished the Monopoly board threateningly.

To be perfectly honest, it *was* just a cunning ploy to get them to stop attacking me. But now that I'd had the thought, there *might* just be something in it.

'Look at it like this,' I said quickly. 'We decided that we'd get Auntie married off and now she's married to Mr Arora – I mean, Uncle Jai.'

'What's your point?' asked Geena suspiciously.

'Then there's Molly Mahal,' I went on regardless. 'We helped her too, didn't we? She's a big Bollywood star again now, thanks to us.'

Molly Mahal was another of our projects that had turned out amazingly well. She was a Bollywood actress who'd been down and out and living in Reading, but we'd helped her get her career back on track (I've got a *lot* more to tell you about Molly Mahal later).

'And don't forget Kiran. We helped her through a bad time after her dad died, and now she's a good mate. And then there's Baby and Rocky. We got them together, didn't we?'

'A match made in *me, me, me* heaven, that one,' Geena remarked.

'I'm getting bored,' Jazz said, opening and snapping the Monopoly board shut dangerously close to my nose. 'What, if anything, are you trying to say, Amber?'

'I'm reminding you how many people's lives we've been a very important part of,' I said, quite lyrically. 'How many hearts we've touched. How many futures we've changed.'

'As far as I recall, we got Rocky and our bimbo-brained cousin together to keep him out of the way at Auntie's wedding,' said Geena, 'to make sure he didn't get a chance to perform his gruesome rap music.'

Jazz and I both shuddered at the memory.

'Well, that in itself was a challenge,' I pointed

out. 'And that's what I'm trying to tell you. Maybe we need a *new* challenge.'

Geena and Jazz didn't look at all convinced.

'We need a project that's going to use all our enormous intelligence, skills and creativity to the full,' I went on, getting quite carried away, the more I thought about it. 'Well, mine anyway, as I'm the ideas person around here.'

'Your ideas, Amber, have got us into more trouble than I care to remember,' Geena retorted, rather too forcefully, I felt.

'So you want a new project, Amber?' Jazz repeated thoughtfully.

I nodded.

'A new challenge?'

I nodded again.

'Well, here's one,' Jazz went on gleefully, staring out of the bedroom window. 'George Botley is walking up our garden path right now. And he's wearing a shirt and tie.'

'*What?*' I shrieked.

I bounced across the bed, shedding a few more bits of Monopoly along the way, and peered outside. George Botley was indeed marching towards our front door in a very determined fashion. He was wearing our school tie with a shirt and jeans. Not a good look. I don't want you to get the wrong idea about George Botley. Not at all. He's in my class at school and he has a thing for me, but I don't encourage him. Not *ever*.

I flung open the window. 'George!' I whispered, hoping Dad hadn't already spotted him from the living room. Or Auntie from the house next door. It was a dark November evening, but there was a streetlight just outside our house, and anyway, Auntie has eyes like a hawk and radar like a bat. 'What are you *doing* here?'

'Oh, hi, Amber.' George beamed up at me. 'I've come to ask your dad if I can take you to the movies.'

'What fun!' Geena chortled, scrambling over to peer out of the window. Jazz followed, sniggering very annoyingly.

'George, I already *told* you,' I said through gritted teeth, 'my dad doesn't allow us to go out with boys.'

'I know,' George replied, 'that's why I thought I'd come and ask him properly. That's why I've put a shirt and tie on.'

'It's your school tie,' I pointed out.

'I know, it's the only one I've got,' George explained. 'I was going to borrow one from my dad, but he's only got the black one he wore to my gran's funeral.'

I rolled my eyes while Geena and Jazz muffled their giggles.

'George, you really ought to keep away from my dad,' I said. 'He's more dangerous than he appears at first glance.'

George raised his eyebrows. 'He was nice to me at your auntie's wedding,' he pointed out.

'George, Dad *seems* very nice,' I said, 'but in reality he's not like that at all. Underneath that mild-mannered exterior, he's a raging tiger.'

Geena and Jazz were in fits on the floor by now.

'I really think you should go home, George,' I went on firmly. 'We'll talk about this at school on Monday.'

George looked disappointed. 'OK.'

I sighed with relief as he wandered off down the street. 'Once again, Amber's lightning-quick brain gets her out of a dodgy situation,' I said with pride.

'Only until Monday,' Geena retorted. 'It *does* seem strange that George is so stuck on you, though. The poor deluded boy obviously needs specialist help.'

'Why don't you just ask Dad if you can go out with George, and get it over with?' Jazz asked.

'Because I don't *want* to go out with him, that's why,' I said. Although I suppose I *was* fond of

George in a way. Kind of like you might be fond of a pet gerbil. 'I don't want to go out with *anyone*. Can you imagine the stress of trying to keep it a secret from Dad and Auntie?'

Jazz nodded agreement. 'Auntie would find out. That woman knows *everything*.'

'Exactly,' I said. 'And we all remember what Dad said about dating. We're not allowed to go out with a boy until we're sixteen, and then Dad or Auntie will be going along with us.'

'Which means we're going to end up living together as three old unmarried women, arguing about Monopoly until we die,' Jazz said glumly.

'You're being extremely quiet.' I turned to Geena. 'Anything you want to share with us?'

I was kind of joking around, but Geena looked me straight in the eye and very slowly turned pink. Always a sure sign of guilt.

'Me?' she said in an over-casual voice. 'Like what?'

'Ooh! What *have* you been up to, Geena?' Jazz demanded, pouncing like a piranha. 'Have *you* got a boyfriend?'

'No, I haven't!' Geena snapped, rather too aggressively. Which instantly made me more suspicious.

Jazz and I glanced at each other and nodded.

Then we both fixed Geena with a glassy, un-blinking stare. That always used to freak her out when we were kids.

'I do *not* have a boyfriend!' Geena yelled.

'OK, have you *had* a boyfriend?' I probed.

'I have friends who happen to be boys,' Geena parried.

'Oh, stop messing about,' Jazz said. 'What we want to know is – has any kissing taken place?'

'Stop staring at me like that,' Geena said irritably, stalking over to the door. 'And don't ask ridiculous questions. Of course I've never had a boyfriend, and I've never kissed a boy either.'

She went out of the bedroom and the door banged shut behind her.

'She's definitely had a boyfriend and she's definitely kissed him,' said Jazz, glowing with excitement. 'This is *huge!*'

'Hold on a moment,' I replied, beginning to collect up the Monopoly pieces from the floor. 'We don't have any proof yet. It's obviously our sisterly duty to find out if it's true or not. But we'll take it slowly, all right?'

Jazz rubbed her hands together gleefully. 'Oh, the possibilities for blackmail are endless!' she sighed.

'Why don't you give me a hand?' I suggested, sweeping up a pile of banknotes.

'Are you mad?' Jazz yawned. 'Let Geena clear it up. It's her bedroom. Anyway' – she glanced at the clock – 'it's nearly time for *Who's in the House?* We can't miss *that*.'

'No way. It's just getting interesting.'

So I dropped all the Monopoly pieces on the carpet again and the two of us clattered downstairs. As we reached the hall, Auntie came out of the kitchen, carrying a plate piled with samosas.

'What have you two been saying to Geena?' she asked without preamble. 'She's sitting in front of the TV with a face on her that would stop a clock.'

'Nothing,' Jazz said, slightly overdoing the wide-eyed innocent bit.

'Auntie, don't you *ever* get tired of *noticing* things?' I remarked. 'Don't you ever wonder how much more peaceful your life would be if you just stopped worrying about other people and only thought about yourself?'

Auntie smiled. 'What a lovely idea, Amber. Unfortunately that's never going to happen with you three around.'

Geena was sitting on the sofa in the living room with a sulky look on her face that could have stopped any number of clocks. Uncle Jai – he was

Uncle at home and Mr Arora at school – was arranging bowls of popcorn and bottles of cola on the coffee table. He and Auntie often came round from next door to watch *Who's in the House?* with us.

'AND NOW,' boomed the TV in the corner, making us all jump, *'whatever you do, DO NOT LEAVE THE ROOM! DO NOT CHANGE CHANNELS! Because if you do, you'll miss the programme everyone, but everyone, is talking about! WHO'S IN THE HOUSE? Next, after the break!'*

Who's in the House? was one of those awful reality shows that everyone moans about, but absolutely *everyone* watches. Ten people were locked up in a house together for weeks on end, and they had to do various tests and trials. The people who performed the worst in the tests were kicked out, one by one, by public vote. Remember I said I had more to tell you about Molly Mahal? Well, she was one of the contestants taking part in the celebrity version of the programme.

'Go and fetch your dad, Jazz,' said Auntie, placing the samosas on the table.

Jazz didn't move from the armchair where she was comfortably sprawled.

'DAD!' she roared at the top of her voice.

Auntie sighed.

A moment later Dad wandered in, looking distracted, with his glasses perched on his forehead.

'Dad, did you know that underneath your mild-mannered exterior, you're really a raging tiger?' asked Jazz.

'I always suspected it,' Dad replied, taking a samosa.

'Popcorn?' Uncle Jai passed the bowl to Geena, who shook her head.

'I don't know why we always have to watch this ridiculous programme,' she said tartly. 'I mean, it's not as if any of us *liked* Molly Mahal that much when she stayed with us.'

'Some of us did,' Auntie remarked.

Uncle Jai blushed, but luckily Auntie was smiling.

'Geena's in a teensy-weensy little bad mood at the moment,' I said. 'She's got a lot on her mind.'

Geena glared at me.

'Like school work, I hope,' said Dad.

'Of course,' Geena replied hurriedly.

'I wonder if Molly Mahal's going to win,' said Jazz, which was the same remark she'd made every single night since the programme started.

Auntie tutted disapprovingly as the ad break finished. 'Geena's right though, it really *is* ridiculous. It's about time the TV companies started making more worthwhile programmes.' Auntie said this every night too, but she still watched, along with the rest of us. 'Do we *really* want to see Z-list celebrities in skimpy outfits crying, fighting and swearing at each other?'

'I'm not complaining,' said Dad and laughed, which is what *he* did every time.

The rap music that always began the programme was now blaring out (*Wh-o-o-o-o-o-'s in da house!*) and then the presenter, Kieron King, loomed out of the screen and began yelling at us:

'*Welcome to the Friday night edition of WH-O-O-O-O-O'S IN THE HOUSE?! Tonight's eviction night, folks, and this very night, one of our celebrities will LEAVE the house and WALK THE WALK OF SHAME!*'

The crowd of people standing around Kieron King whooped and yelled and jumped up and down, while making sure that they jostled their way in front of the camera so they could wave to their mums back home. Behind them was the gaudy *Who's in the House?* building, which looked like a toy house made of colourful building blocks.

'Why do they always have to talk so loudly?' Uncle Jai asked with a frown. 'We're not deaf.'

'It's because they think the viewers might fall asleep otherwise,' Auntie replied.

The programme had been running for a few weeks now, and there were only six contestants left of the original eight. These were: Molly Mahal, an ex-England and Chelsea footballer called Steve Kelly, the obligatory has-been pop singer Luke Lee, TV presenter Shannon Pickering, and Romy Turner, a model who seemed to be there only because she had a very large chest. The last contestant was Katy Simpson, who wasn't a celebrity at all but had once been married to someone who was famous.

We already knew that Shannon Pickering and Kim Simpson had performed the worst in the week's trials, so they were the two who might be voted out tonight. The Friday night programme was actually quite dull because all that happened was that they showed clips of the previous week's trials before announcing the loser at the end.

'I'm going to vote for Shannon,' Jazz said, whipping out her mobile as the telephone number appeared on the screen. 'She whines all the time. I hate her.'

'You can't hate someone you don't know,' Auntie pointed out quite reasonably.

'And I'm not paying your phone bill this month,' Dad added. 'You'll be paying it yourself out of your pocket money.'

Jazz, who had already voted about fifty times this week, put her mobile away, looking disgruntled.

'Anyway, the programme makers edit what they film to make some of the contestants look worse than others,' Geena said as we watched Molly Mahal trying to knit with spaghetti, which had been part of Tuesday's *Pasta Pranks*. 'I mean, look at Molly. They obviously *love* her.'

Molly was laughing as her spaghetti slipped off the knitting needles, making sure her stunning profile was to camera. She always seemed to get the best camera angles and the best lighting. She never swore or misbehaved or showed too much naked flesh (unlike Romy Turner). Ever since the programme started, the newspapers had been full of stuff about how 'lovely' and how 'natural' Molly was. She was apparently the favourite to win it too.

'You know, I never thought Molly was a good actress,' I remarked, 'but considering what a snooty madam she was when she stayed with us, she's doing a great job here.'

'Maybe she had a personality transplant when she had all that other cosmetic surgery done,' Geena suggested.

We all stared at Molly's wider eyes, slimmer

nose, unwrinkled brow and bigger bosoms.

'Geena's right, you know,' Auntie agreed. 'The programme makers have their own agenda. I mean, I thought Shannon's penne pasta model of the Eiffel Tower was quite good, but she didn't get many votes for it.'

'That's because everyone hates her,' said Jazz.

As the programme moved on to Wednesday's tightrope-walking challenge, I found my mind wandering. Geena and Jazz often remark that it doesn't always come back again, ha ha. *So* not funny.

I hadn't forgotten what I'd said upstairs. I had quickly become convinced that life was a bit too quiet around here since Auntie had got married and moved out.

It was up to me to liven things up, just a little.

Chapter Two

'I *told* you Shannon would lose,' Jazz said with satisfaction as we set off for school early on Monday morning. 'I'm so glad. I really hate her.'

'Yes, I think we get that,' Geena replied. 'It looks like Molly might win, although Romy Turner got a lot of votes for last week's trials.'

'That's not surprising,' Jazz remarked, 'seeing as she did them all in her itsy-bitsy silver bikini.'

'Fascinating as this conversation is,' I butted in, 'I do have something a little more interesting to discuss with you.'

'I doubt it.' Jazz sniffed. 'But go on.'

'About what I was saying on Friday evening,' I began.

Geena and Jazz stared blankly at me.

'You know, about life being a bit dull at the moment,' I reminded them impatiently.

'Oh, that.' Geena shrugged. 'As this is probably going to involve one of your daft ideas, Amber, you can count me out.'

I smiled. 'Well, maybe I'll just have to do something on my own then. Like detective work, for instance. Finding out if anyone's got any secrets they don't want Dad or Auntie to know about . . .'

'What did you have in mind?' Geena asked hastily.

'Well—'

'Hey! Wait for us!'

We turned to see Kim and Kiran scooting along the street towards us. Kim and I have been friends ever since we first went to school and I stopped George Botley painting her blue. We've only known Kiran since the beginning of term, when she moved to our town. We didn't really get off on the right foot (to be completely honest, she actually shoved a newspaper down my school jumper) but since then we've become good friends.

'Did you see *Who's in the House* on Friday night?' Kim panted as they finally caught us up. 'Wasn't Molly great? I think she's going to win, you know.'

'I was so glad Shannon got kicked out,' Kiran added. 'I really hated her.'

'Oh, and me,' Jazz said. 'I hated her too.'

'For God's sake!' I groaned. 'Are we so shallow that some dumb TV programme is all we can talk about?'

Kim raised her eyebrows at me. 'And what's the matter with you today?'

You'd never believe that Kim used to be really sweet and quiet. Now she asserts herself all over the place. I blame Auntie – oh, and Molly Mahal. She gave Kim expert lessons in how to be a diva when she was staying with us.

'Amber thinks our life is too boring,' Jazz explained. 'She thinks everything's settled down too much since Auntie got married.'

'Oh no!' Kim pulled a face. 'This sounds like another of Amber's bird-brained schemes.'

'My schemes are anything but bird-brained,' I replied with dignity. 'All I'm saying is—'

'Ooh, look over there!' Jazz broke in, grabbing my arm. 'It's Baby and Rocky.'

Our cousin and her boyfriend were standing on the corner at the end of the street. Rocky was in Geena's year but Baby went to a private school nearby (her parents, Uncle Davinder and Auntie Rita, were seriously rich). The private school's uniform consisted of a black skirt, white shirt, black and gold striped tie and a gold sweater.

Baby had the skirt pulled up about fifteen centimetres above her knee, the tie was nowhere to be seen and the top three buttons of her shirt were undone. She had the sweater tied round her waist, and she was carrying her coat (designer, naturally) even though it was a chilly autumn morning.

'Oh, what a surprise.' Geena yawned as, frowning furiously, Baby stepped forward and poked Rocky hard in the chest. 'They're arguing as usual.'

'Baby's going to walk away in a minute,' Jazz predicted. 'Five, four, three, two – there she goes!'

Baby had spun round on her impossibly high Vivienne Westwood stilettos and stalked off down the road. Meanwhile Rocky stomped off in the opposite direction.

'What *is* it with those two?' asked Kiran.

'What, apart from the fact that they both have a hugely inflated opinion of themselves, gigantic egos and no brains?' said Geena. 'Not much, really.'

'There you go, Amber.' Jazz nudged me in the ribs. 'You could help Baby and Rocky improve their relationship.'

'I don't think even *my* talents could stretch *that* far,' I said modestly. Geena, Jazz, Kiran and Kim all sniggered. Highly uncalled for. 'Anyway, Baby and Rocky seem to *enjoy* arguing.'

'What about poor, lovesick George Botley?' Jazz asked with a gleam in her eyes as we joined the throng of kids swarming through the school gates. 'He definitely needs help.' She turned to Kiran and Kim. 'He came round to our house on Friday night to ask Amber on a date, you know.'

Kiran and Kim laughed heartily at this.

'Ooh, tell us more!' Kim said eagerly. 'We want to know all the details! What did your dad do? What did Auntie say?'

'Nothing,' I snapped. 'He didn't get that far. Anyway, I have other plans for George Botley.'

'Really!' Jazz exclaimed. 'And do these plans involve *kissing*?'

The four of them shrieked with laughter and made kissing sounds at me.

'Not at all,' I said haughtily. I had indeed come up with a very good plan for dealing with George Botley, and I was about to tell them all about it when someone tapped me on the shoulder.

'Hey, you!'

I turned to see one of the sixth-formers, a boy called Gareth Parker, glaring at me through thick-lensed, black-framed glasses. He was accompanied by another sixth-former, Soo-Lin

Pang, who looked equally stern. She was carrying a clipboard.

'Yes?' I said coldly. To be honest, I was surprised to see sixth-formers in the main part of the playground. They had their own very posh and spacious building set apart from the rest of the school, so they didn't come and mix with lowly scumbags like us very often. We all hated them because they thought they were so cool, but all the same we were jealous of their luxurious building with its huge common room and kitchen.

'Trainers,' snapped Gareth, pointing his pen at my feet.

'Oh, this is a word-association game, right?' I said. 'You say trainers, and I say – um, laces?'

Gareth flushed. 'Don't try to be funny, Amber,' he snapped. 'Soo-Lin, read the rules about trainers, please.'

'*Coppergate pupils are allowed to wear trainers, but these must conform to school rules,*' Soo-Lin read from her clipboard in a monotone. '*They must be dark in colour and in good condition. Football boots are not acceptable footwear in school.*'

I glanced down at my flash neon-pink Nike trainers with metallic purple bits. 'Well, they're in good condition and they're not football boots,' I offered. 'Two out of three isn't bad.'

'What's it got to do with you, anyway, Gareth?' Geena put in belligerently.

Gareth fixed her with a stony stare from under his floppy black fringe. 'Mr Grimwade has noticed that school uniform standards are slipping,' he said coldly. Mr Grimwade was the deputy head and was always making a nuisance of himself. 'So he's asked some of the sixth-formers to do uniform checks every morning.'

'I might have known Grimwade would be behind this,' Geena muttered.

'*Mr* Grimwade to you,' Gareth retorted with another piercing glare. 'And while we're on the subject, Geena, your earrings are too big.'

We all stared at Geena's large silver hoops.

'Ha!' Geena said triumphantly. 'That's where you're wrong, actually. I checked the rules, so don't bother asking your tame little sidekick here to read them out.' Soo-Lin looked mortally offended. 'Hoops can be up to three centimetres in diameter, and mine are *exactly* three centimetres. So there.'

'Go, Geena!' said Jazz, and we all applauded.

'I'll be the judge of whether your earrings are acceptable or not,' Gareth said pompously. He held out his hand. 'Soo-Lin, the tape measure, please.'

Muttering under her breath, Geena unhooked one of her hoops and slapped it down in Gareth's outstretched palm. Meanwhile Soo-Lin was looking mutinous.

'Can't I do this one, Gareth?' she pleaded. 'I never get to do any measuring.'

'You can do it next time,' Gareth said impatiently.

'You know, you really need to get out more,' I told Soo-Lin as she reluctantly handed Gareth the tape measure.

'You're right,' she sighed. 'This is the most excitement I've had for weeks. My parents expect me to study all the time and they don't like me going out, even at weekends—'

Gareth tutted loudly. 'When you've *quite* finished . . .' He drew out the tape measure with a flourish and carefully measured Geena's earring. 'Three point two centimetres,' he announced with immense satisfaction.

'What!' Geena shrieked. 'No way.'

'Two millimetres over?' Kiran raised her eyebrows. 'Hardly worth making a fuss about, is it?'

Gareth looked slightly nervous. Kiran's big and square and she has a tongue stud. In fact, she looks quite hard. She could probably flatten a weedy swot like Gareth with one hand.

'Just make sure you don't wear either those trainers or those earrings again,' Gareth warned, backing away a little. 'Soo-Lin, make a note to check on Amber and Geena tomorrow.'

'Are you sure you'll have time?' Geena snapped.

Gareth looked confused. 'What?'

'Well, surely you should be spending your time looking for a life, as you clearly don't have one at the moment,' Geena riposted superbly.

Blushing, Gareth slunk away, muttering something to Soo-Lin who was trying very hard not to giggle.

'What a complete prat,' I commented. 'And look, Gareth's not the only one.'

There were indeed lots of sixth-formers with clipboards bullying other hapless kids in various parts of the playground.

'They're power-mad, that lot,' said Kim. 'Hey, Amber, if you're bored, how about teaching some of these snooty sixth-formers a lesson?'

'Yep, that sounds like fun,' I agreed. 'I'll think about it.'

'So you were about to tell us what you're going to do about George Botley?' Jazz asked nosily.

I smiled. 'Ever heard of the Labours of Hercules?'

Kim and Jazz looked totally blank.

'He was an ancient Greek hero who had to perform ten tasks, for some reason,' said Kiran. 'I can't remember why.'

'He had to kill various creatures like a lion, a boar and a snake with lots of heads,' Geena added. 'Oh, and he had to clean all the muck out of a huge stable. That was one of the tasks.'

'How utterly non-fascinating,' said Jazz. 'And what does all this have to do with George Botley?'

'All right, forget Hercules,' I said. 'Even the ignorant amongst us, like Jazz and Kim, must have read those old fairy tales where a handsome hero has to perform a series of tasks in order to win the hand of the fair princess?'

'Of course,' Jazz replied. 'But George Botley isn't a handsome hero and you aren't a fair princess by any stretch of the imagination.'

I ignored her. 'Well, that's what I'm going to do,' I went on. 'I'm going to set George some tasks and tell him he has to be successful if he wants to impress Dad and Auntie and take me on a date.'

They all sniggered.

'Look, it's just to keep George occupied for a while,' I explained. 'Anyway, if he's got any sense, he'll tell me politely to get lost and go and pester someone else. That's what I'm banking on.'

'I wouldn't bank on him having *any* sense, actually,' Kim remarked. 'After all, he fancies *you*, doesn't he?'

'Ooh, here's George now!' Jazz hopped up and down gleefully. 'And he's coming over!'

'This I simply have to see,' said Geena.

George was grinning from ear to ear. I thought the presence of the others might put him off, but he didn't seem the slightest bit fazed.

'Hey, Amber,' he called, strolling towards me. 'You said we were going to have that talk today.'

'Yes, George, I did,' I said solemnly, 'and here's the deal. You have to prove to my dad and to Auntie that you're worthy of a date with me.'

Muffled giggles all round.

'So I thought it would be fun if I set you a few tasks to complete,' I went on. 'Dad and Auntie won't let me date just any old person. So you have to prove that you're serious and committed.'

'What, that my intentions are honourable, you mean?' George said with a wink.

'Something like that,' I replied. 'Of course, I completely understand if you don't want to do it . . .'

George mulled it over for a moment. 'OK,' he said easily. 'It sounds like a bit of a laugh. What do you want me to do first?'

I was stunned. 'Excuse me?'

'My first task,' George said. 'What do you want me to do?'

'Yes, Amber,' said the other four helpfully, like some annoying Greek chorus. 'What do you want him to do?'

Oh, blast. I hadn't actually thought of anything as I'd been reasonably sure that George would tell me to get lost.

'Oh – ah – well . . .' I glanced around for inspiration and my gaze fell on the canteen on the other side of the school. 'Your first task, George, if you choose to accept it, is this – get me into lunch before everyone else in the lower school. For a whole week.'

George looked shocked and there was a sharp intake of breath from the others. The queue for the canteen was always a complete scrum. There was supposed to be a shift system, but the dinner ladies were helpless, and it was everyone for themselves.

'Of course, if you don't think you can . . .' I let my voice tail away, shrugging my shoulders.

'I'll give it a go,' George said, and he trudged away, frowning.

'A whole week, mind,' I called after him. 'If you

don't manage a whole week in one go, then we have to start over again.'

'You're quite heartless, Amber,' said Geena with admiration. 'He'll probably get trampled to bits trying to clear a path to the front of the queue for you.'

'Well, it should keep him busy for a good few weeks,' I said cheerfully. 'And then I've got lots more ideas for *new* tasks.'

The conversation moved back to more idle gossip about *Who's in the House?*, and while we were chatting, my gaze strayed idly over to the opposite side of the street. The old Coppergate School had been completely demolished, and builders were preparing the site to build houses. Our new school was swish and flash and very posh, but Mr Morgan, the headteacher, was still trying to bully us into doing loads of sponsored events to raise money for extra refinements. Local businesses had donated plenty of cash too, and they'd had parts of the school named after them. For instance, the canteen was now officially named the Bolton Canteen (Bolton's Best Biscuits), although no one ever called it that, despite Mr Grimwade constantly reminding us. The drama studio had also received a large injection of cash from Mackenzie Allan, a local accountancy firm, and was now called the Mackenzie Allan Studio.

Then it hit me. All of a sudden, full in the face, right between the eyes. *Wham!*

'Listen to me, all of you,' I announced breathlessly. 'I've just had one of my best ideas *ever*.'

Chapter Three

Sad to relate – and unbelievable too – Geena, Jazz, Kiran and Kim continued discussing Romy Turner's trout pout without taking the slightest notice of me.

'Didn't you hear what I said?' I demanded.

'Of course,' Jazz replied. 'Didn't *you* realize we were ignoring you, you silly girl?'

'But – I've just had the *most* fantastic idea!' I protested.

'Oh, yippee.' Geena yawned. 'Time for me to go and find my mates. See you, guys.'

'Hold it right there!' I said sternly. 'This concerns you too, Geena.'

'Bye, Amber,' Geena retorted.

'It's about Mum.'

Geena immediately turned back. 'What *about* Mum?'

I didn't answer. Instead I flung out my arms. 'Look around you. The Bolton Canteen. The Mackenzie Allan Studio. The SuperSports Gym.'

'You've missed out the Kingston Medical Room,' said Jazz. 'And it seems like you should be heading straight there yourself.'

'They're all named after big businesses who've donated money to the school,' I swept on regardless. Honestly, if I responded to every insult hurled at me, we'd be here all day. 'What about if we could get something at Coppergate named after Mum?'

There was silence. I had been glowing with excitement but now I suddenly felt unsure of myself as still no one said anything.

'I think I just saw a pig flying across the sky,' Geena said faintly. 'For once, Amber has *actually* had a truly great idea.'

'I agree,' said Jazz, smiling widely. 'A memorial for Mum, here at Coppergate. It's *brilliant*.'

'That's a fabulous idea, Amber,' Kim said, patting me on the arm. 'I'll help you any way I can.'

'Me too,' added Kiran.

'All right,' I said briskly, blinking very hard because I felt a *teeny* bit teary. 'So we're agreed then.'

'But where do we start?' Jazz asked.

'And will Mr Morgan go for it?' Geena added, looking a bit doubtful.

'I can't see Morgan turning down free money,' I replied confidently. 'And I was thinking about the library. If we could donate some money to the school, then Mr Morgan might agree to rename the library after Mum.'

'The Anjleen Dhillon Library,' Geena said thoughtfully. 'Mmm, sounds good.'

The library in our new school was about three times the size of the old one, and Mr Morgan had been making noises for some time about doing more fund-raising to buy extra books and new furniture. The problem was that now everyone, teachers and pupils alike, ran a mile every time the words *sponsored event* were mentioned.

'Of course, we'll ask Dad for the money,' Jazz said.

'Of course we won't ask Dad for the money.' I eyeballed her sternly. 'We'll raise it *ourselves*.'

'But how?' Geena enquired. 'Everyone's sick of sponsored events.'

'Ours will be different,' I assured her as the bell for morning lessons pealed out. 'Anyway, the first thing to do is speak to Mr Morgan and see what he says.'

'Actually, the first thing we need to do is *find* Mr Morgan,' Geena pointed out. 'If he exists at all. You do know that there's rumours he's left and been replaced by a hologram?'

'OK, so he doesn't seem to be around school much,' I agreed. 'But there's his car.' I pointed at the sleek silver Jaguar in the teachers' car park. 'So he must be here this morning.'

'Let's go right now!' Jazz said eagerly.

Kiran and Kim went off to class with instructions to let Mr Hernandez, my borderline-lunatic form tutor, know where I was. Mr Morgan's office was in the quietest part of the school, a good distance away from the classrooms. I sometimes wondered if Mr M. actually *realized* that he was a headteacher at all. He always seemed to be out attending meetings, and as he was leaving next term anyway, he was around even less than before.

Mr Morgan's office door was shut and the neon sign above it had been switched from AVAILABLE to ENGAGED.

'If you ever see it on AVAILABLE, I'll give you a fiver,' said Jazz.

I raised my hand. 'Shall I just knock anyway?'

'Girls! What *are* you doing?'

Mrs Capstick, the school secretary, had popped

her head out of the office next door and was giving us the evil eye.

'We just wanted to speak to Mr Morgan,' I said apologetically, feeling like a criminal mastermind caught in some dastardly act.

Mrs Capstick clicked her tongue reprovingly. 'Now, now, girls, you know you have to come and see me to make an appointment.'

'Well, what's the point of that then?' Jazz asked, looking up at the sign.

Mrs Capstick ignored her. She ushered us into her office and opened a large blue diary.

'Now let me see,' she said, tapping her pen against her teeth. 'Is it urgent?'

'It's a matter of life and death,' I said.

'Well, I *might* be able to fit you in next week,' Mrs Capstick went on thoughtfully. 'Mr Morgan has ten minutes or so after lunch on Wednesday.'

'Next Wednesday!' Jazz exclaimed. 'But that's *ages*—'

'That'll be fine,' I said quickly.

Mrs Capstick wrote our names down in the diary and we wandered out.

'Maybe Mr Morgan has a secret life as a super-hero,' Jazz suggested. 'That's why he's never in school. He's too busy saving the world.'

'Oh, stop,' said Geena. 'I've just had this

horrible image of Mr Morgan in a lycra costume.'

'And on that ghastly note, I'll see you two later,' I added. 'Start thinking up some fund-raising ideas – and they've *got* to be *really* different from anything that's been done in school before.'

We split up at the end of the corridor and went our separate ways. On the way to my form group, I began mentally ticking off fund-raising events. Sponsored walks, runs, spelling bees, silences, sleepovers, readathons . . . The list was endless. But *our* fund-raising was going to be *special*.

I didn't know how yet, but it was.

'Ah, there you are, Amber,' Mr Hernandez said as I entered the classroom. His blue shirt patterned with swaying hula girls was loud, even for him. 'I'd given you up for dead.'

'Not quite, sir,' I replied. I sat down next to Kim and Kiran. 'Guess how long we have to wait to see Mr Morgan.'

'Got to be next week at the earliest,' Kiran said. 'Thursday?'

'Close.' I shrugged. 'Wednesday.'

'Well, you can start fund-raising right away,' Kim pointed out. 'You don't have to wait to see Mr Morgan. What are you going to do first?'

'Kim, these things take time,' I said with

exasperation. 'It's got to be thought about and properly planned.'

'You mean you don't know,' Kim replied with annoying promptness.

'What I mean is, I'm working on it,' I said.

I worked on it all through the morning when I should have been studying maths, science and French. By lunch time I had a long list of possible fund-raising events. Unfortunately I'd crossed the whole lot out. They were all too *ordinary*. Too dull. We needed something that would fire everyone's interest and make them give us loads of money. *But what?*

'God, I'm starving,' I said as Kiran, Kim and I went across the playground towards the canteen. Although the lunchtime bell had literally only rung out about thirty seconds before, there was already a hungry crowd stretching right along the corridor, baying for food. 'How *do* these people manage to get to the front of the queue so quickly?'

'It must be particularly bad today,' Kim remarked. 'Look, Mrs Openshaw is on guard.'

Mrs Openshaw was the cook. She'd started at the school a few weeks ago, but she was the only one of the dinner staff who was scary enough to make people behave. When she said you had to have vegetables, *you had vegetables*. She was broad and tall, looming over the younger kids like a bottle-blonde giantess, and occasionally when the queue got too rowdy, she'd stomp out, brandishing a wooden spoon. She was standing there now, glowering at everyone.

'Hey, Amber, there you are.' George Botley was at my elbow. 'Come on. Mrs Openshaw's waiting for you.'

'Me!' I laughed. 'Don't be ridiculous.'

'She *is*,' George insisted. 'She's going to let you into lunch first.'

I stared at him in bemusement.

'The task you set me!' George rolled his eyes impatiently. 'Remember? I spoke to Mrs Openshaw, and she's going to let you in early for lunch every day this week. Just like you wanted.'

I was stunned into silence. But Kim and Kiran made up for that by shrieking with laughter and holding each other up very theatrically.

'George,' I spluttered, 'you're not *serious*?'

'Yoo-hoo, Amber!' Mrs Openshaw was waving her wooden spoon at me. 'Over here, dear.'

'Go on.' George poked me in the back.

'But – but – *how*?' I groaned.

'Mrs Openshaw's a big fan of *Who's in the House?*' George explained, looking very smug.

'And she loves Molly Mahal. I told her you'd get her autograph for her.'

'George!' I wanted to put my hands around his neck and deprive him of air. 'I can't do that! I don't even know how to get in touch with Molly.'

That wasn't strictly true. Molly had left us the name and address of her agent when she moved out, but I wasn't going to tell George *that*.

'Oh, well.' George shrugged. 'You can tell Mrs O. that *after* the week's over. Ha ha!'

I looked at Mrs Openshaw and gulped. She was staring fiercely at the kids at the front of the queue. 'Stand aside,' she boomed. 'Stand aside, I say!'

A gap opened in the crowd like Moses parting the Red Sea. With great ceremony George escorted me to the head of the queue, leaving Kim and Kiran chortling gleefully behind us. I burned with embarrassment as I ran the gauntlet of glares and grumbles from everyone else who had been in front of me.

'Enjoy your lunch, Amber,' Jazz said bitterly. She was fourth in the line with her friends Shweta and Zoe.

'Look, I didn't know George was going to do this,' I wailed, but I was bundled inside the canteen by Mrs Openshaw. George stood just inside the doorway, grinning all over his stupid face, until the crowd closed in on him and shunted him out of the way.

'I do love Molly Mahal.' Mrs Openshaw nipped back behind the serving hatch, where the other canteen staff were watching us in amazement. 'I can't believe she used to live with you before I started at Coppergate. Trust me to miss all the excitement.' She picked up a plate and began piling carrots onto it. 'You'll have cabbage and cauliflower as well, Amber.'

It was a statement, not a question. As I carried my heavy plate over to the table and sat down on my own, the rest of the queue glaring at me through the windows, I realized that I had made a very, very serious mistake.

I had completely underestimated George Botley.

'I suppose you expect us to let you out of the play-ground gates first.' Jazz sniffed as we left school that evening.

'Oh, stop,' I said. I had been teased without mercy all afternoon, and I was feeling rather fragile. 'Look, I didn't know George was going to pull that off.'

'Well, he did, and rather spectacularly too,'

Geena observed. 'And *you're* going to have to carry on all week now, Amber.'

'I think I should warn you that you might actually suffer some kind of serious injury,' Jazz said helpfully. 'Feelings were running rather high in the lunch queue after you swept past us with your nose in the air.'

'I so did not do that,' I retorted. 'Anyway, I told George and Mrs Openshaw that once was quite enough.'

'So is Mrs Openshaw going to get her Molly Mahal autograph as a reward?' Kim enquired.

'Well, I was thinking of forging it,' I admitted.

Jazz, Geena, Kim and Kiran stared sternly at me.

'Oh all right, I'll write to Molly,' I muttered. 'But it could be ages before I get a reply. *Who's in the House?* doesn't finish for another couple of weeks.'

'Hey, Amber.' George Botley materialized at my side, looking very satisfied with himself. 'Enjoy your lunch?'

'Yes, thanks,' I snapped, against a backdrop of sniggers and giggles from the others.

'Bet you didn't think I'd manage it,' George said in a jaunty tone.

'No, I didn't,' I agreed. At that precise moment we were passing the teachers' car park; I saw Mr

43

Morgan's silver Jaguar again and an idea popped swiftly into my head. 'George, I have another task for you.'

'Cool.' George cocked his head and looked at me expectantly.

'Geena, Jazz and I need to see Mr Morgan urgently,' I went on. 'Get us an appointment before next Wednesday.'

George looked astounded and this time *I* was the one who felt satisfied. *That* had shut up the sniggers and giggles.

'No way!' George shook his head. 'That *is* impossible.'

'Nothing's impossible, Georgie,' I said, wagging my finger playfully at him. 'I'll wait for you to get back to me.'

And I strode off, leaving George apparently deep in thought.

'Amber, you're quite, quite ruthless,' Jazz said with grudging admiration as she and the others scuttled along behind me.

'Why?' I shrugged. 'If by some extraordinary unparalleled miracle, George *does* manage to get us an earlier appointment with Mr Morgan, it'll be all to the good.'

'But he won't,' Kiran predicted.

I smiled wolfishly. 'Then I shall make him pay

the penalty. As for you two' – I eyeballed Geena and Jazz – 'don't rely on *me*, outrageously creative as I am, to come up with all the fund-raising ideas. Tomorrow we'll have a meeting. And I shall expect each of you to have thought up at least one utterly fantastic plan to raise loads of money.'

Geena looked down her nose at me. 'Honestly, Amber, I can see you ending up as the tinpot dictator of some minor South American country.'

'Oh yes, there aren't many career choices for someone like Amber,' Jazz agreed. 'What about the villain in James Bond films whose aim is always world domination? That's the *ultimate* in bossiness.'

'Look, this is for *Mum*,' I pointed out. 'I'm not going to pull any punches.'

Geena and Jazz were silent. They looked a bit worried. Secretly, I was also slightly concerned. I was realizing that it wasn't *easy* to come up with spectacular stunts that would raise hundreds of pounds, just like that. For the first time in the last two years, I began to feel a little sorry for Mr Morgan and his never-ending attempts to raise cash to pour into the bottomless money-pit that was Coppergate School . . .

We didn't tell Dad, Auntie and Mr Arora about

our idea until we were all together, waiting for that evening's *Who's in the House?* to start. I put the TV on mute, stood in the middle of the living room and cleared my throat.

'I have something to say.'

'What have you done now?' Auntie enquired. 'I already know it was you who broke the microwave.'

'It was an accident,' I replied quickly. 'Anyway, did you know that if Jazz hasn't got any clean socks on a school morning, she washes out yesterday's pair and dries them in the microwave? *That* can't be good for it.'

'What?' Geena shrieked, dropping the pakora she was holding. 'You mean we're eating food that has shared a microwave with *Jazz's socks*?'

'Oh, you are so dead, Amber,' Jazz muttered.

Auntie and Dad raised their eyebrows at her.

'We'll be having a chat about the importance of planning ahead and being organized after the programme, Jasvinder,' Dad said sternly.

'As well as a l-o-n-g lesson on how to use the washing machine,' Auntie added.

'Anyway,' I said, having neatly deflected the question of *how* I accidentally broke the microwave in the first place, 'this is about Mum.'

There was instant silence, and Dad, Auntie and

Uncle Jai looked intrigued. Quickly I outlined our plan.

'And so we want to raise enough money to get the school library named after Mum,' I finished up. 'What do you think?'

I didn't dare look at Dad. I know what he's like.

'Girls, that's a wonderful idea,' he said in a choked voice. 'I know your mum would be very proud of you—'. He stopped.

'Don't cry, Dad,' said Geena. 'You'll start us all off.'

'I think it would be a fantastic way to remember your mum.' Auntie smiled warmly at us, and Uncle Jai nodded.

'We'll all help in any way we can,' he said.

'And if anyone can bully and browbeat people into giving lots of money, it's you three,' Auntie added.

'Thanks,' I said.

'It *was* a compliment,' replied Auntie.

'And just to start off your fund-raising, I'll give you a donation.' Dad looked from me to Geena and Jazz. 'Shall we say a thousand pounds?'

'Oh, Dad, thanks!' We all threw ourselves at him and had a group hug.

'We won't have much fund-raising to do *now*!' Jazz said gleefully as we disentangled ourselves.

'Er – maybe you'd better wait and see how much money Mr Morgan will want you to donate,' Uncle Jai suggested.

'It won't be a problem.' I waved my hand airily. 'We can do this!'

'Well, you can sit down and shut up for now, Amber.' Jazz dived for the remote control. 'It's time for *Who's in the House?*'

At that very moment the telephone rang.

'Oh, really!' Jazz said crossly. 'Who could be so inconsiderate as to ring at the exact second *Who's in the House?* starts?'

Dad went out to answer it while we watched the recap of Shannon Pickering being kicked out, much to Jazz's glee.

'Sorry, got to pop out.' Dad poked his head round the door. 'It's that big engineering project we've got on at work. One of my colleagues needs some help.'

'How even more inconsiderate,' Jazz grumbled. 'You're going to miss the programme now, Dad.'

'Record it,' Dad instructed, 'and I'll watch it later.'

Dad left, and we watched as the remaining five contestants were told their trial for the day, which involved balancing jellies on various parts of their anatomy. Classy.

'Oh my God!' Romy Turner squealed dramatically through her obviously fake, cushion-like lips. 'I'll never be able to do *this*!'

'Don't worry,' Molly said, sliding a comforting arm around her, 'I'll help you.'

Jazz, Geena, Auntie and I groaned.

'Why wasn't she that sweet when she stayed with us?' Jazz remarked.

'Oh, come now, girls,' said Uncle Jai. 'She wasn't *that* bad.'

'You wouldn't know,' Auntie retorted – a bit tartly, I thought, for someone who'd only been married a few weeks. 'You're a man.'

'Yes, thank you for clearing that one up,' Uncle Jai said.

Auntie's eyes narrowed slightly. I tried to turn a little so that I could look at both of them while pretending to watch the TV. Geena and Jazz were doing the same, Jazz almost tying herself into a knot like Kaa the python in Disney's *The Jungle Book*.

'All I'm saying—' Auntie began. Then she stopped abruptly as she noticed three pairs of ears flapping like clothes on a washing line. 'Jasvinder, is there something wrong with your neck?'

'No,' Jazz muttered, uncoiling herself.

Auntie jumped to her feet as the first ad break

began. 'I'll get some more crisps,' she snapped.

She stalked out. We all turned and stared at Uncle Jai.

'And I'll just go and help your auntie – er – open the crisp packet,' he said feebly and hurried off.

'Well!' Jazz said in a stage whisper. 'What was *that* all about?'

'You know how Molly always flirted like mad with Uncle Jai when she was here,' I reminded her. 'Auntie probably still gets a bit wound up about it.'

'But we've been watching the show for ages now, and she's always treated it as a joke before today,' Geena pointed out. 'What's changed?'

'I don't know,' I replied, feeling a little worried. 'But something's just not right.'

Chapter Four

'Hey, Amber!'

As we went through the school gates the following morning, someone called out my name. I spun round, half expecting to see Commandant Gareth and his henchwoman Soo-Lin. I'd changed my trainers, but I'd carefully chosen a blue pair, the colour of which was mid-way between dark and light. I felt quite satisfied as I contemplated the many arguments I could have with Gareth about whether my trainers were dark enough to comply with school rules. Geena, however, had rebelliously stuck with the same hoops, declaring that she'd just whip them out of her ears if she saw Gareth coming.

But it wasn't Gareth at all. Instead George Botley came ambling towards us.

'Hi, George,' I called. 'Come to update me on

your plan to get us an appointment with Mr Morgan?'

'I don't have a plan,' said George.

I smiled sympathetically. 'Well, never mind, George. The main thing is never to give up and to keep on trying. You know the old saying, don't you? *try, try and try again If at first you don't succeed*—'

'No, you don't get it,' George broke in. 'There *is* no plan because I've already done it.'

'WHAT!' I yelled. Geena, Jazz, Kiran and Kim were too stupefied even to laugh.

'Mr Morgan says he'll see you today straight after the lunch bell,' George explained patiently. 'But you'll have to be quick because he's only got about five minutes.'

'But . . .' I was opening and closing my mouth like a fish gasping for air.

'I'll just pretend you've said thanks then, shall I?' George asked, looking a teeny bit miffed.

'Oh, wait a minute.' I was beginning to recover my composure. 'I get it. We turn up at lunch time and Mr Morgan has "unexpectedly" had to go out. Nice try, George.'

'I'm disappointed in you, Amber,' George replied, raising his eyebrows. 'Mrs Capstick has written it down in the diary. Go and ask her.'

I stared at him uncertainly. 'But – but – I don't understand!' I wailed. 'How? When? Mr Morgan's never here, and when he is, he's never available!'

George shrugged. 'It was easy,' he replied. 'I waited in the car park last night until he came out of school.'

We all goggled at him.

'Well, he had to come out sometime, didn't he?' George pointed out. 'I only had to wait about half an hour.'

'And?' I interjected faintly.

'He was pretty surprised to see me,' George went on. 'But I'd polished his car with my jumper while I was waiting, so he was dead impressed. I asked him if he had a few minutes today to see you and he said yes, and sent me back into school to tell Mrs Capstick.'

'How brilliantly straightforward,' Geena murmured. 'The kind of simple idea you couldn't even begin to get your head around, Amber.'

George looked rather offended. 'Are you saying I'm a bit simple?'

'Not at all, George,' Geena assured him. 'We're all mightily impressed with your intelligence and tenacity. Especially Amber.'

Geena, Jazz, Kiran and Kim all turned to stare

at me. Now that they'd got over the initial surprise, they were smirking horribly.

'Yes, very well done, George,' I said with as much dignity as I could manage. 'Now I think you should take a short break before I give you your next task. We don't want you overdoing things.'

'OK.' George winked, but I think it was more at the others than at me. Then he strolled away. I had a rather gloomy feeling that although I'd thought I was getting the better of him, George was *actually* getting the better of me.

'He's beating you hands down, Amber,' Jazz remarked gleefully. 'I'm starting to like him!'

'Me too,' said Geena. 'This daily humiliation of Amber by George Botley is really livening up the school day.'

'Well, prepare for your own daily dose of humiliation,' I replied. 'Gareth Parker is heading straight towards us.'

With a shriek of surprise Geena clapped her hands over her ears, hiding her hoops from view.

'He's staring at your trainers, Amber,' Kiran said as Gareth and Soo-Lin homed in on us.

'I'm looking forward to this.' I had been formulating my arguments all morning and was completely prepared to compete with Gareth in a battle of wits.

'I'm glad to see you've changed your trainers, Amber,' he said, and then turned immediately to Geena, leaving me furious and sulking. 'Let me see your earrings, please.'

'No.' Geena looked defiant, hands still clamped over her ears.

Gareth looked nonplussed. 'Geena, remove your hands please.'

'No,' said Geena. 'And you can't make me.'

The rest of us broke into whoops and cheers, and a curious crowd began to drift towards us from other parts of the playground.

'Stop acting like a five-year-old,' Gareth ordered, 'or I'll tell Mr Grimwade!'

'Who's the five-year-old *now*?' Geena snapped.

They faced off for a moment and then Gareth, red-faced, stomped away without another word. Soo-Lin scuttled after him. Everyone standing around us broke into spontaneous applause.

'You'd better take the hoops off, just in case he *does* tell Grimwade, Geena,' I cautioned.

'He wouldn't dare,' Geena replied, flushed with victory.

The bell rang just after that, and the morning began. I have to admit, I didn't *totally* believe George until we went to the school office at lunch time. Mrs Capstick was at her computer when we tapped and went in.

'Er – we have an appointment to see Mr Morgan,' I said apologetically, half expecting her to jump to her feet, denounce us as charlatans and liars, and throw us out.

'Ah, yes.' Mrs Capstick glanced at the diary. 'I'll just make sure he's free.'

She led us across to the connecting door that opened into the headteacher's office. There we all paused and Mrs Capstick put her finger to her lips. Then she knocked ever so gently on the door.

'Come,' called Mr Morgan.

We made a move forward, only to be stopped in our tracks by a *look* from Mrs Capstick. She put her head round the door, still keeping us firmly at bay.

'It's the Dhillon girls to see you, Mr Morgan. But I can send them away if you're busy.'

We rolled our eyes at each other.

'No, no, show them in,' said Mr Morgan, to our relief.

Mrs Capstick stepped back and majestically threw the door wider open. I rushed forward, desperate to get in there, Jazz and Geena breathing down my neck. I just hoped the phone didn't ring while we were there and make us lose our precious five minutes.

Mr Morgan – tall and thin and wearing his famous, permanently harassed expression – was seated at his desk. His computer was switched on and he was surrounded by many hundreds of bits of paper.

'Hello, girls.' He took off his spectacles and laid them on the desk. 'What did you want to see me about?' He sounded mildly surprised that *anyone* should want to see him.

'Well, it's like this, sir,' I began, and I launched into the speech I'd prepared. I'd timed myself, and if I gabbled at top speed, I could get through it in about twelve seconds.

'. . . and so if you could tell us how much money we'd need to raise, we'd like to go for it,' I finished, gasping for breath, 'and have the library named after our mum.'

Mr Morgan looked very interested, which pleased me.

'Well, I *was* planning on trying to raise the money through donations from local businesses, but I must say, I think this idea shows a lot of initiative on your part, girls,' he said, nodding his approval. 'However . . .'

My heart sank.

'We have a slight problem with timing,' Mr

Morgan went on. 'Have you girls ever seen the TV programme *Class Act*?'

'*Class Act?*' Jazz repeated. 'Oh, you mean that dull schools quiz that's just for swots, nerds and freaks?'

'The very same,' Mr Morgan replied dryly. 'We've applied for a Coppergate team to take part. If we're selected, filming will take place in our library next term so we must have it looking good for the TV cameras.' He steepled his fingers together and eyed us solemnly over them. 'That means I was really hoping to have the library set up with new furniture and books by Christmas.'

'But that's only about six weeks away,' Geena said in dismay.

'No problem,' I cut in confidently. 'We can do it. So' – I lowered my voice like a gangster in a film – 'how much money are we talking about, sir?'

Mr Morgan looked rather pained. It seemed as if he didn't much like talking about cold hard cash, although he didn't mind spending it.

'I'll write it down for you.' He reached for a piece of paper. 'Just remember that this is only a nominal amount,' he went on, scribbling down some figures. 'We'll make up the rest of what we need from the school fund, and I'm sure the PTA will be generous too.'

He handed the paper to me. As I unfolded it, I secretly hoped that it would be a *little* bit more than Dad's generous donation of one thousand pounds. I really wanted to raise a good deal of the money ourselves. It would be something we could do for Mum.

I opened up the paper. *£10,000*, I read.

I just about managed not to drop down in a dead faint on the spot. Swallowing slightly, I passed the paper to Geena.

Geena's eyes widened a little but she managed to keep cool. 'Oh, right,' she muttered, passing the paper to Jazz.

'TEN THOUSAND POUNDS!' Jazz yelled. 'We couldn't *possibly* raise that much!'

'In that case—' Mr Morgan began.

'No, sir, we can do it,' I said with confidence I dredged up from *somewhere*. 'And we'll do it by Christmas.'

'Amber, are you stark staring mad?' Jazz demanded as we left Mr Morgan's office in a daze. 'We'll *never* get that much money, even with Dad's donation – and by Christmas too!'

'Look, I want this as much as you do, Amber,' Geena added. 'But Jazz is right. It's impossible.'

'Nothing's impossible,' I said, while secretly battering my brains to work out exactly how we were going to find this *colossal* amount of money. Mr Morgan had also said that he would inform Mr Grimwade, the deputy head, to tell all the teachers to give us any help they could in raising the money. But *still*. *Ten thousand pounds*.

'Of course some things are impossible!' Jazz snapped. 'Climbing Mount Everest in high heels is impossible. The England football team winning the World Cup is impossible. But those things are *more* possible than us raising ten thousand pounds by Christmas.'

'That's you all over, Jazz,' I jibed as we went out into the playground, where Kiran and Kim were waiting for us. 'You always want to give up at the first hurdle.'

'This is not a hurdle!' Jazz yelled, giving me a shove. 'It's a great big five-metre brick wall!'

'Don't be a wuss!' I shouted, flicking her ear.

'Stop it, you two!' Geena ordered. 'You're both as bad as each other.'

Jazz and I turned on her and we began slapping ineffectually at each other in a very girlie way.

'It went well then, I see,' Kim remarked, coming over to us with Kiran.

'Like a dream,' I replied sourly. 'Morgan said

yes as long as we can raise ten grand by Christmas.'

Kiran and Kim burst out laughing, then stopped dead at the looks on our faces.

'Sorry, we thought you were joking,' Kiran apologized.

'OK, so how exactly are you going to do that?' asked Kim in a very business-like manner.

'Yes, Amber,' Jazz eyed me sulkily. 'How *exactly* are we going to do this?'

'All we need is a plan,' I said. 'One – or maybe a couple – of *really* excellent and original fund-raising ideas. Then we're away. And no' – I held up a hand as everyone opened their mouths at once – 'I *don't* have any ideas yet.'

'In that case, why don't you just start off with something small?' asked Kim. 'What about a yard sale?'

'*A yard sale?*' I screeched, my voice rising about two octaves with indignation. 'Kim, we have to raise *ten thousand pounds*. We need a grand design. A master plan. A sure-fire money-spinner.'

'Well, you won't raise *any* money unless you actually do something,' Kim pointed out with maddening superiority. 'You could still be think-ing about your "grand plan" while you do the yard sale.'

Geena nodded at me. 'Kim's right, Amber. We have to start *somewhere*.'

'I agree,' said Jazz.

'And you three have got enough stuff to sink the *Titanic*,' Kim added. 'You could probably raise quite a bit of money by selling some of it off.'

'Well, OK,' I said in a disgruntled voice. 'You've bullied me into it. We'll have a yard sale this Saturday.'

'You could make it more interesting by turning it into a challenge,' suggested Kiran. 'You know, seeing which of you can make the most money.'

'Like it!' Jazz said, perking up visibly. 'I'll win.'

'In your dreams,' I retorted. 'I shall be making more money than either of you two.'

'How very childish,' said Geena. 'I think my tough bargaining skills will win the day. Not that I shall actually be competing, of course.'

'Oh, of course not,' I scoffed.

Now that we had something to do, even if it *was* something as ordinary as a yard sale, it gave me a bit of a boost. We had an art lesson that afternoon, and as Kim and I finished our pencil sketches of 'Fruit Bowl with Bananas' a bit early, Miss Bonney allowed us to start making posters for the yard sale. At the end of the school day, I rolled them up to take home to finish.

'Let's hurry,' Jazz said impatiently as I met her and Geena at the gates. 'I want to get home and start turning out my bedroom for the yard sale. I'm going to blow you two suckers out of the water!'

'Jazz, we are meant to be in this *together*,' Geena reminded her. 'But if you want to be so silly about it, I'll gladly take you on – and beat you.'

'Eat my dust!' I informed them, taking off at top speed. I wanted to get home ahead of them and sort out *my* bedroom. Then there were all sorts of interesting boxes and bags up in the loft. I was sure I would find saleable items up there. And if I got to Dad and Auntie first, I could ask them for donations too.

Dad was never home from work before us, but Auntie sometimes popped over from next door to cook for us in the evenings. As I let myself in, Geena and Jazz were still pounding down the road calling out insults behind me. The house was warm and the delicious smell of baking scented the air.

I shut the door behind me and then, as an after-thought, put the safety chain on. Giggling to myself, I dropped my bag and raced upstairs. While Jazz and Geena were struggling to get in, I'd make my first foray into the loft and have a good rummage around . . .

Pulling off my school tie, I chucked it through the open door of my bedroom as I ran past. What I saw in there was so terrifying, so horrible, I skidded to a halt and almost fell back down the stairs head over heels.

Baby – yes, Baby, our one and only bird-brained, self-obsessed cousin – was sitting on my bed.

Chapter Five

'B-Baby!' I spluttered, wondering if I was seeing things. Well, *hoping* I was. 'What the hell are you doing in *my* bedroom?'

'Oh, it's yours, is it?' Baby yawned and flicked over a page of the magazine she was reading with one long, crimson, acrylic fingernail. 'I thought there was a funny smell in here.'

Downstairs I could hear Geena and Jazz banging on the door and making threats through the letterbox.

'I said, what are you *doing* here?' I advanced further into the bedroom, only to find my way blocked by three massive suitcases. 'What are *these*?'

Footsteps came rushing up the stairs and Geena and Jazz burst in, followed at a rather more leisurely pace by Auntie. She must have come in through the back door, and then let Geena and Jazz in. There was hardly space to move now with those ginormous suitcases stuck in the middle of the room.

'Ha! Very funny, Amber!' Jazz said savagely. Then she took in the spectacle of Baby perched on my bed, and stopped short, as did Geena. Baby yawned again, looking more bored than ever.

'What's *she* doing here?' asked Geena, eyeing Baby up and down. Our cousin had already changed out of her uniform and was wearing a white silk shirt and figure-hugging skinny jeans, which made me, for one, feel like a swotty frump in my school clothes.

'And hello to you too,' Baby said, raising one perfectly arched and pencilled eyebrow.

'Baby's staying with you for a while,' Auntie explained. 'Her mum and dad have had to go to India very suddenly on business connected with their company.'

'She's staying with *us*?' I repeated, glancing aghast at Geena and Jazz. They both pulled a face at me while Baby smirked and flipped over another page of her magazine.

'Why can't she stay with you and Uncle Jai next door?' Jazz grumbled. 'You've got loads more room than us.'

'Because they've just got married and they want to be on their own,' Baby interjected, staring down her pretty little nose at Jazz. 'I would have thought even an airhead like you would know that. Duh!'

'*I'm* an airhead?' Jazz spluttered, hardly able to contain herself. '*I'm* an airhead?'

'Glad you agree,' Baby said, still smirking.

'Girls!' Auntie said calmly. 'Stop this, please. You have to live together for the next six weeks—'

'*Six weeks!*' I exclaimed, reeling backwards in horror.

'So let's start as you mean to go on,' Auntie carried on, ignoring me.

'We already have,' Jazz muttered.

'Anyway, why has Baby got *my* room?' I enquired. 'I *always* have to move out when someone new moves in.'

'Because you have *slightly* less stuff than Geena and Jazz, so it's easier for you to move, Amber,' Auntie explained patiently.

That reminded me.

'Auntie, we're going to have a yard sale here on Saturday and I was wondering—'

'If you had any spare stuff—' Geena interjected swiftly.

'*That I could have to sell on my stall!*' Jazz yelled, muscling in at the finish.

I turned on the two of them. 'I asked first!'

'No, you didn't!' Geena snapped.

'Please, Auntie,' Jazz wheedled, taking a different tack. 'I'll load the dishwasher for a whole week.'

Auntie smiled. 'I take it there's some kind of competition going on here?'

I explained about the yard sale and the contest to see who could raise the most money.

'I'll sort out some things for your stalls,' she agreed. '*But*' – she held up her hand as we all opened our mouths to stake a claim – 'I'll be dividing them fairly between the three of you. Understood?'

We all nodded sulkily.

'*A yard sale?*' Baby sounded as disgusted as if someone had told her to clean the toilet with her toothbrush. 'How very uncool.'

All three of us turned on her.

'It's for a great cause,' Geena said frostily. 'The library at school is being renamed after our mum, and we're giving a donation.'

'Yes, and we're raising almost all the money ourselves,' I added.

'Ten thousand pounds,' Jazz snapped, glaring

at Baby. 'What do you think of *that*, then?'

'I think a *yard sale* isn't going to raise anywhere near that amount of money,' Baby pointed out. 'What you need is a really good money-spinning idea. A master plan. A—'

'Yes, we know,' I interrupted sullenly.

'Amber, start moving some of your things into Geena's room before dinner,' Auntie instructed me. 'You can sort out things for your yard sale while you're doing it.'

'*My* room!' Geena repeated with horror. 'Why can't she move in with Jazz?'

'No-o-o-o!' Jazz wailed. 'I shared with Amber when Auntie came here, *and* when Molly Mahal moved in. It's your turn, Geena.'

'But I need my space!' Geena proclaimed melodramatically. 'I have GCSE coursework!'

'Oh, stop moaning and get on with it,' Auntie said, and went out.

'Thanks for the warm welcome, Geena,' I said, making a great show of squeezing my way past Baby's gigantic suitcases. 'I'll start collecting my stuff and be over to yours right away. And don't worry if you have any *secrets* you don't want anyone finding out about. I won't say a word, I promise . . .'

Looking rather fraught, Geena disappeared

abruptly along the landing. I smiled to myself. I hadn't forgotten about the possibility of her having a secret boyfriend – I just hadn't had much time to investigate yet. But maybe moving into her bedroom would give me the perfect opportunity. Jazz had obviously realized this too, because she winked knowingly at me as she went out.

'What's going on?' asked Baby, nose twitching like a bloodhound. 'What's Geena up to?'

'Why are *you* so interested?' I asked, opening my wardrobe. It was stuffed to the seams and I was sure I had plenty of clothes I could sell on my stall.

'Well, I've got to find *something* to make the next six weeks a bit more fun.' Baby lay back and lounged on my bed. She was still wearing her red stiletto shoes. 'I don't suppose Auntie will let me go out in the evenings, will she?'

'Got it in one,' I replied, beginning to sort through the clothes rail.

'Well, do you think she'll let Rocky come round?'

'She might.' I held up a Gap denim skirt I hadn't worn for ages. 'But you can forget any hanky-panky. Snogging and such-like will be strictly out of bounds.'

'Oh, great. Just great.' Baby flopped back sullenly onto the pillows. 'You can get rid of that stripy tank-top, by the way, Amber. Those are *so* out this season.'

I gritted my teeth and did not reply. I'd only bought it last Saturday.

By dinner time I'd made a pile of clothes, shoes and trainers for my stall. I'd added books, games and bits of make-up and anything else I could find. But I still wasn't satisfied. I needed more. I'd *never* raise more money than Geena and Jazz with just this stuff.

'You'll *never* raise more money than Geena and Jazz with just this stuff,' Baby said, picking up a pink pleated skirt and staring at it disdainfully.

'I haven't finished collecting things yet,' I replied, wondering how long it would be before one of us murdered Baby and hid her corpse under the bed.

Dad was working late on his engineering project again, so Auntie and Uncle Jai came over to have dinner with us. They didn't always when Dad was out, but I guessed that tonight they were playing the same role as a United Nations peace-keeping force.

'So how are all you girls getting along?' asked Uncle Jai as we sat down at the table.

There was a grim silence.

'They'll be fine,' Auntie said. There was an edge to her tone which made it clear that we *would* be fine, or else. 'Baby's our guest, and she's very welcome. Have some salmon, Baby.'

Baby pulled a face. 'I don't like fish.'

'You should,' Jazz said. 'It's brain food. Perfect for you.'

Baby looked offended. She and Jazz eyeballed each other across the table.

'There's some chicken in the fridge,' Auntie said.

'Oh, can I have a stir-fry?' asked Baby sweetly. 'It's nice and healthy. I don't want to get *fat*.' And she stared pointedly at Geena, who was serving herself chips. Geena, who's *not* fat but rather curvy, looked furious and put four chips back.

Auntie glanced down at her own dinner, which she hadn't even started on, sighed slightly and got up.

'Baby's our guest, remember?' I told her.

'Don't push it, Amber.' Auntie disappeared into the kitchen.

'I can't believe Dad's working late again,' Jazz grumbled. 'He worked late all last week too.'

'It's because his firm's working on that big project,' I reminded her.

'Maybe he's got a girlfriend,' Baby suggested idly, nibbling on a slice of cucumber.

'What!' Jazz howled. 'Don't be ridiculous!'

Baby smiled.

'Would you like a spoon, Baby, as you seem determined to do quite a bit of stirring,' I said calmly. I was quite cool about it, unlike Jazz, who looked as if she wanted to plunge her fork into Baby's arm.

'Now, now, girls,' said Uncle Jai in his teacher's voice.

'Six weeks living with *her*,' Jazz moaned as we adjourned to the living room after dinner to watch that evening's episode of *Who's in the House?* 'How can this be possible? I feel ill.'

'It's freezing,' Baby complained loudly. 'Do you ever have the heating on or are you just too poor?'

'The timer should be switching it on round about now,' Auntie replied in a clipped tone. 'Have you been watching *Who's in the House?*, Baby?'

'Ooh, *yes*,' Baby said enthusiastically. 'I just love Steve Kelly. He's *gor*geous!'

I rolled my eyes at Geena and Jazz. Steve Kelly, a Premiership footballer, seemed determined to be a complete stereotype. He boasted continually about all the money he earned and the cars he owned, and spent most of his time leering at Romy Turner in her bikini. I guessed that Baby's ultimate ambition in life was probably to be a WAG.

'And what about that old has-been Molly Mahal?' Baby went on. 'Hello, major plastic surgery alert!'

'OK, so she's had a bit of help in the looks department,' I said sharply, 'but she's very popular. Everyone thinks she's going to win.'

'Why are *you* standing up for her?' Baby yawned, slumping into the comfiest armchair, which was also in the best position for viewing the TV. 'She was completely snooty and obnoxious when she stayed here.'

'Remind you of anyone?' Jazz muttered in my ear as Baby shivered theatrically.

'Can I have a cup of coffee, please?' she asked in a *poor little me* voice. 'That might warm me up a bit.'

'I'll get it,' Uncle Jai said quickly after one glance at Auntie's face.

'By the way, how much stuff have you two got for your stall?' Jazz asked, looking from me to Geena.

'Oh, lots,' said Geena guardedly.

'Loads,' I replied. 'And that reminds me. Kim

and I started making some posters this afternoon. We can finish them off after *Who's in the House?'*

I ran upstairs to get the posters. On the landing there was a large bookcase, crammed with books and a hundred other different things. As I passed by, I caught sight of a silver sunglasses case perched on top of a pile of books.

I stopped and opened the case up. Jazz's Calvin Klein sunglasses were inside. They'd been her favourites once upon a time, but then she'd bullied Dad into buying her some Gucci shades for her birthday and she'd never worn the CK ones since, as far as I could remember . . .

'What are you doing, Amber?' Baby was peering through the banisters at me. I hadn't heard her come up the stairs.

'Nothing,' I said, sliding the sunglasses neatly behind my back.

'I need my cashmere jumper, I'm freezing,' Baby complained. She went into my bedroom and I heard her banging her suitcases about. Meanwhile I hurried into Dad's room: I'd decided to hide my stash of stall goodies under his bed, away from the prying eyes of Geena and Jazz.

I shoved Jazz's sunglasses under the bed and sat back on my heels, flushed with satisfaction. Oh, come on, of course I wasn't *stealing* Jazz's sunglasses. Not at all. If she mentioned that they were missing before the yard sale, then I'd hand them over straight away. No question. But I'm sure she doesn't want them any more. They've been sitting on that bookcase for at *least* six months.

Anyway, you know the old saying.

Finders keepers, right, girls?

'Is it going to be like this *every* morning for six weeks?' Jazz asked in a superbly tragic tone as we trudged off to school the next day. 'What *are* we going to do?'

Baby had outdone herself. First she'd spent an hour in the bathroom and used up all the hot water. Then she'd managed to burn a hole in my bedroom carpet with her GHD hair straighteners. She wanted toast and orange juice for breakfast and we didn't have any OJ so Auntie had to run to Mr Attwal's minimarket. And then go back for low-fat marge because Baby doesn't eat butter. All this before eight o'clock too.

'Baby's acting like J-Lo,' Geena grumbled. 'All these diva-ish demands.'

'Just be grateful we can get away from her at school,' I pointed out. Baby was so late leaving this morning that she'd bullied Dad into giving her a lift (the school was ten miles away from Dad's workplace, in the opposite direction and through some of the most hellish commuter traffic in the history of western civilization). Apparently Baby 'didn't do buses'.

'Do you know, she even told Dad not to drop her off in front of the school.' Geena sniffed disapprovingly. 'She said it's not good for her image to be seen getting out of a car that isn't a Mercedes.'

'I thought Molly Mahal was a complete pain in the behind when she stayed with us,' Jazz remarked, 'but Baby's a hundred times worse.'

'Speaking of Molly Mahal, I think she almost cracked last night for the first time,' I said. 'Did you catch that look on her face when they announced that she was up for eviction this week?'

Who's in the House? the night before had ended in uproar. The remaining five contestants had, as usual, been given a silly challenge. This time they'd been asked to cut each other's hair into certain styles. This sounded hilarious until we found out that they were going to be wearing wigs so no one's *actual* hair was going to be affected at all. What a con.

Anyway, they all chose their wigs and put them

on, and then they hacked each other about, and it *was* quite funny. Molly cut Luke Lee's (he's the has-been pop star), and his wig actually looked a lot better than his own hair.

Then had come the shocking announcement that this week we, the public, weren't going to be voting for the two people who'd done worst in the week's trials so far (Jazz had her phone in her hand ready to vote for Romy Turner, who'd made Steve Kelly's head look like a lop-sided pine-apple). Instead the contestants were told to look inside their wigs as two of them had notes hidden in them. These notes said: *You are nominated to leave the house this week.* Molly Mahal got one and Steve Kelly got the other.

'It's *such* a fix,' Geena said. 'The programme makers know that everyone's going to vote to keep Molly in because they love her so much. Cue lots of phone votes and lots of lovely money for the TV company.'

'I wish she'd gone ballistic and torn the house apart,' Jazz said wistfully. 'That's what I was hoping for.'

'She did look a teensy-weensy bit annoyed for about half a nanosecond.' I remembered the expression that had flashed across Molly's face before she went into her *Oh, well, never mind, I never expected to win anyway, I'm just so happy I got this far* routine. 'She's definitely got some sort of master plan going on.' Molly Mahal was a survivor who always looked after Number One. I knew that for a fact.

There was hardly anyone around in the playground when we arrived at school. I'd texted Kim and Kiran to tell them we were coming along early to put up the posters about the yard sale and not to wait around for us later.

'We ought to spread them out across the playground,' I said, unrolling the ones I'd made. They were quite tasteful – large black stencilled lettering on a pale pink background: YARD SALE AT THE DHILLONS' HOUSE, and then the date. Very stylish.

'Dear me, Jazz, yours are a bit garish,' Geena remarked as Jazz unrolled her own posters. She'd used loads of gold sequins and silver glitter and she'd also cut out pictures of celebrities and stuck them on there too. One of them was Molly Mahal, next to the head of Victoria Beckham.

'Well, yours and Amber's are boring,' Jazz retorted. 'We need some glamour and excitement to make people come along and buy our goods.'

'So are you two selling loads of your designer stuff then?' Geena asked curiously.

'Me?' I said innocently. 'No, of course not. Only a few things I don't want any more.'

Which was true enough. I wasn't going to mention that I'd added two of Geena's Abercrombie & Fitch T-shirts and a pair of Jazz's Nike trainers to the rapidly expanding pile of goodies under Dad's bed. I mean, these things were just lying around the house, doing *nothing*. Geena and Jazz obviously didn't *want* them.

'I'm selling a few of my designer things too,' Jazz added, tying one of her posters to the gate. 'And there are loads of my old toys in the loft. I think I might try selling those—'

'You there! What are you up to?'

Geena's face darkened. 'It's him again!' she hissed.

Gareth Parker was charging across the play-ground towards us, clutching a clipboard.

'Oh, hello, Commandant – I mean, Gareth,' I said. 'Where's your little sidekick today?'

'If you mean Soo-Lin,' Gareth snapped, 'she's not in today. She's sick.'

'Of you?' Geena enquired sweetly.

Gareth went red, eyed Geena's earrings and obviously decided to leave that battle for another day. Instead he turned on Jazz.

'What are you doing?'

'Preparing to land my spaceship on the moon,' Jazz replied calmly, tying the last corner of her poster in place. 'What does it look like?'

'Do you have permission to put these posters up in the playground?' demanded Gareth.

'Yes, we do,' I said, not missing a beat. 'We have permission from the Big Cheese himself, the King of Coppergate School, the one and only Mr Morgan.'

This was stretching a point, I admit. But Mr Morgan had said how pleased he was that we were showing initiative, so I was *almost* sure he wouldn't mind. Besides, if Gareth wanted to check with him, it could take weeks. Ha ha.

'I'd invite you to come along to our sale, Gareth,' Geena remarked, 'but unfortunately for you, we won't be selling charisma and personality.'

Jazz and I giggled.

'I didn't think you would be,' Gareth retorted. 'After all, you've hardly got any to spare, have you?'

And he marched off, leaving Geena with her mouth open.

'You and Gareth *really* don't like each other, do you?' Jazz said.

'Never mind that idiot,' Geena muttered. 'Let's get these posters up.'

We distributed the posters around the play-ground and were just putting up the last ones when George Botley appeared at my shoulder.

'Hey, Amber, did you see *Who's in the House?* last night?' he asked. 'Reckon Molly will get evicted?'

'George, much as I would love to stand around discussing the merits of poor-quality TV pro-grammes with you, as you can see I'm very busy,' I said pompously.

'Oh, yes, the yard sale.' George peered at Jazz's brash poster and blinked slightly. 'Lucky I got you that appointment with Mr Morgan, wasn't it?'

'Yes, thank you, George, I'm extremely grate-ful,' I said with a sigh. Then a thought struck me. 'By the way, George, are you ready for your next assignment?'

'Yep, the James Bond of Coppergate, that's me,' George replied.

'Don't get above yourself,' I retorted. 'Here's a nice easy one for you. Get as many people as possible to come to our yard sale on Saturday.'

'No probs.' George strolled off, looking smug.

'And don't promise everyone Molly Mahal's autograph this time,' I called after him.

Looking slightly disgruntled, George nodded.

'So how much stuff *have* you two collected for your stalls?' Jazz asked.

'Not much,' Geena said, too quickly.

'Hardly anything,' I said, also too quickly.

'Oh, I believe you, of course,' Jazz scoffed.

By the end of the week I was well pleased with what I'd stashed away under Dad's bed. In fact, I'd had to lock the overspill away in the bottom of his wardrobe. I had some *great* stuff and a lot of it was designer, which meant I could charge higher prices. A lot of it had also once belonged to Geena and Jazz. Well, *please*. If you're going to leave lovely sunglasses and T-shirts and trainers and make-up and perfume all around the house and never use them, you aren't going to miss them, are you?

Auntie had also taken the three of us up into the loft and then refereed the free-for-all scrum that followed. After Jazz and Geena had a tug of war over a handbag that nearly resulted in Jazz falling into the water tank, Auntie had made sure that everything was divided up fairly. I was still convinced, though, that I was going to have the best stall, packed with designer goodies.

It was almost time for the Friday-night edition of *Who's in the House?* to start, and I didn't want to miss it. We'd find out today if Molly Mahal was going to be kicked out. I'd just popped into Dad's bedroom to add a Stila eyeshadow kit to my stash (it was Geena's but she'd never even opened it – what a waste of money!) when, on my way down the stairs, I saw one of Baby's suitcases lying open on my bed. Even though I'd cleared out my wardrobe and chest of drawers for her, Baby hadn't bothered to unpack. My eyes widened at the sight of all the clothes, shoes and make-up spilling out of the case. Even peeking between the banisters I could see Gucci, CK, DKNY, Versace, Armani . . .

'What are you staring at, Amber?' Baby suddenly popped out from behind the door and looked at me suspiciously. She'd changed out of her school uniform and was now wearing a pale pink fluffy sweater, cut-off denims and white sky-high heels. The perfect outfit for lounging around the house watching TV.

'Nothing,' I said. 'It's not illegal to look into one's own bedroom, you know.'

'Depends why you're doing it,' Baby retorted, closing the suitcase with a snap. 'I keep my cases locked by the way. In case you and your sisters are thinking of thieving anything.'

'You've got a nerve—' I began, but the doorbell interrupted me.

'That'll be Rocky.' Baby bounced out of the bed-room and dashed down the stairs, throwing me back against the wall.

'Rocky?'

'He's coming to watch *Who's in the House?* with us,' Baby explained.

I followed Baby down the stairs in time to see Auntie make it to the door three seconds before she did. Auntie ushered Rocky in and then stared pointedly at him as he moved to give Baby a kiss. Rocky panicked, lost it and ended up shaking Baby's hand instead.

'We're all in the living room, Rocky,' Auntie said, taking his arm in a grip of steel. 'This way.'

Rocky was borne away by Auntie, leaving Baby trailing sullenly in their wake. I went down to the living room myself, where Uncle Jai, Geena and Jazz were already waiting. We all sniggered (well, Geena, Jazz and I did) when Auntie put Rocky at one end of the sofa and Baby at the other end. She then sat down in between them.

'This is just like *A Midsummer Night's Dream*,' Geena remarked. 'You know, those lovers Pyramus and Thisbe who can only talk to each other through a hole in a wall.'

Rocky and Baby were now staring yearningly at each other behind Auntie's back.

'Thank you for that, Geena,' Auntie said tartly, leaning back to cut off their view.

The front door banged shut and Dad rushed into the room, dropping his briefcase and loosening his tie.

'Sorry I'm late,' he gabbled. 'Work again.'

'Oh, we thought you might have a secret girlfriend,' Baby said in a poisonously sweet tone.

'How ridiculous,' said Dad. 'What have I missed?'

'Nothing,' Jazz replied as the programme began.

'This rap music is so rubbish,' Rocky complained. 'Why didn't the TV company ask someone like *me* to write the theme music?'

'Ooh, yes, you'd have done a great job, Rocks,' Baby said adoringly. She leaned forward and made silent kissing noises at him until Auntie gave her a look. 'Did you get me that silver bracelet, by the way?'

Rocky shook his head. 'Nah, it was too expensive.'

Baby frowned. 'You *said* you could afford it from your allowance.'

'I know, but I spent the money on something else,' Rocky muttered sheepishly.

'You spent the money on something *else*?' Baby repeated in a truly terrible voice.

'Excuse me, we're trying to watch TV here,' Jazz grumbled.

'It's only a repeat of this week's challenges,' Baby retorted.

'Anyway, I had less money this month because I've lent *you* loads,' Rocky defended himself. 'And you haven't paid me back yet.'

'Ooh, you fibber!' Baby proclaimed indignantly. 'I've only borrowed about ten quid.'

'Thirty-five pounds fifty pence, actually,' said Rocky.

'Auntie, maybe you could knock their heads together and shut them up,' Jazz suggested.

'I *am* quite tempted,' Auntie replied, looking sternly from one to the other. Baby and Rocky both subsided into sulky silence.

We were all quite on edge when the moment arrived to find out who was leaving the house. Molly Mahal had dressed up in a sea-green and silver sari and was looking very calm and composed. But I wondered what she was really thinking.

'I hope Molly gets evicted,' Baby said eagerly. 'She *so* thinks she's it.'

'She's not bad-looking for an old woman,' Rocky remarked.

'Oh, don't be daft,' Baby screeched. 'It's all fake.'

'Who cares?' Rocky shrugged. 'It's better than looking at some wrinkly old hag with everything hanging down to her knees.'

'Will you two shut up!' I snapped, as Kieron King ceremoniously opened the golden envelope. 'We're going to miss it!'

'And the celebrity leaving the house tonight is . . .' Kieron King paused dramatically.

'Anyway, the bracelet didn't cost *that* much, Rocky,' Baby said. 'I bet you could have afforded it if you really wanted to.'

'SHUT UP!' we all shouted. I think even Dad and Uncle Jai joined in that time.

'STEVE KELLY!' Kieron King proclaimed.

'I knew it!' Geena exclaimed. 'I knew Molly wouldn't get voted out.'

'Oh, no!' Baby was looking *very* disappointed. 'I love Steve Kelly. I don't want him to go – he's gorgeous.'

'What do you mean, he's gorgeous?' Rocky demanded. 'Do you mean you fancy him?'

'Well, *duh*,' Baby replied. 'He's good-looking and rich and he's got a great body. What's not to fancy? I bet Steve Kelly wouldn't complain about buying me a measly little bracelet.'

'Do you two *ever* stop arguing?' Auntie enquired.

Rocky and Baby looked amazed.

'This isn't an argument,' Baby said coldly. 'This is a discussion.'

'Yes, an argument's when we throw things,' Rocky added.

Steve Kelly was now emerging from the celebrity house to cheers and applause and a burst of fireworks.

'Looks like you're out of luck, Baby,' Jazz remarked as a tall, blonde, unfeasibly long-legged woman in a very short skirt rushed towards the footballer. 'That's his girlfriend.'

'Ooh, listen, she's having a go at him about flirting with Romy Turner,' said Geena gleefully. 'And look! She's whacking him with her designer handbag.'

I have to say, it was quite an entertaining end to the evening. And of course, I was really looking forward to the yard sale tomorrow. We had Dad's donation, of course. But this would be our first chance to raise some money ourselves.

For our mum.

*   *   *

I stepped back and gazed at my stall with satisfaction. I had done a superb job, if I say so myself. The table was crammed with goodies and I'd labelled everything neatly with prices. It wasn't a warm day but the sun *was* shining and it wasn't raining, which was about as good as you can get in November.

I glanced over my shoulder. Geena and Jazz had set up their stalls in different parts of our garden and I was curious to see how much stuff they had. So I strolled over to Geena's table first. She was just putting the finishing touches to her display.

'Not a bad effort,' I said, 'but quite pitiful compared to mine, really.'

'Shall we just wait and see who makes the most money?' Geena enquired in a bored tone, re-arranging a pair of diamanté and silver earrings at the front of her table.

I did a double take. 'Those earrings!' I yelled, making a grab for them. 'They're mine!'

Geena grabbed too, and she got there first.

'So? You haven't worn them for about six months at least!'

'That's such a lie!' I retorted, trying to wrestle them from her grasp. 'I wore them last week!'

'OK, so where did I find them then?' asked Geena.

'I – er – ah . . .' I was flummoxed.

'See?' Geena said triumphantly. 'You didn't even know where they were!'

'Wait a minute . . .' Jazz had come over to see what was going on. Now she was staring wide-eyed at a pair of pink shoes that had pride of place in the middle of Geena's stall. 'Those shoes are mine, Geena, you thieving little weasel!'

'Oh, get over yourself!' Geena snapped. 'You don't even wear them.'

'I want them back!' Jazz launched herself at the stall but Geena blocked her path.

'Hey! What's *that*?' A green skirt hanging on Jazz's table had caught my eye and I dashed over there, leaving Geena and Jazz fighting over the shoes. 'Jazz, you sly little toad!' I yelled, taking in the contents of her stall in one glance. 'You've nicked loads of my stuff!'

Geena, who'd managed to repel Jazz's attack by now, burst out laughing.

'I don't know what you're laughing about, Geena,' called Jazz, who'd sprinted over to take a look at my table. ' *'Cos Amber's nicked heaps of your stuff.'*

'WHAT!' Geena screeched. 'Amber, I'm going to kill you!'

'And good morning to you too.' Auntie

stepped out of the back door, followed by a smirking Baby. 'I see you've all found out what's been going on.'

'You mean – you knew?' Jazz gasped.

'It was obvious to anyone with half a brain,' Baby added with smugness.

'You mean you *have* half a brain?' Geena snapped. 'You hide it well.'

Auntie shrugged. 'None of you even realized that anything was missing,' she pointed out. 'Which just goes to show that you all have too much stuff anyway.'

Baby had come over to look at my stall. Under my astonished gaze, she swiftly picked out five of my best designer items (including three belonging to Geena and Jazz) and opened her purse.

'I'll have these,' she said briskly. 'And get a move on, I want to look at the other stalls before the customers turn up.'

'I'm not selling to you!' I spluttered.

'Why not?' Baby demanded.

'Yes, why not?' Auntie chimed in, hardly bothering to hide a smile. 'Baby's money is as good as anyone else's.'

Still smirking, Baby held out twenty pounds. I snatched it grumpily and then she swept over to Geena's stall.

'Oh, by the way, I came round to tell you that there's a lot of people in the driveway,' Auntie went on, 'and the queue goes halfway down the street.'

'What!' I couldn't believe my ears. I dashed over to the wooden gates at the side of the garden and peered through a large crack.

As Auntie had said, the driveway at the side of the house was full of people. I could see Kim and Kiran, and my other friends from school, Chelsea and Sharelle. I also spotted Jazz's mates, Shweta and Zoe, and Geena's friends, Kyra Hollins and Hinnah Muteen. But there were also quite a few people I didn't know at all.

'Hi, Amber.' A face appeared on the other side of the crack. I shrieked with fright and jumped back.

'It's only me,' said George Botley. 'Told you I'd get a load of people to come, didn't I?'

'And how did you manage it?' I asked, trying not to sound too impressed.

George chuckled. 'I told everyone that you, Geena and Jazz were selling off all your designer stuff,' he said. 'OK, maybe it was a bit of a fib, but there was almost a riot to be first in the queue this morning.'

'George, it's not as much of a fib as you think,' I said bitterly.

'Oh, right.' George peered through the crack at me. 'Hey, Amber, remember that bit in *A Midsummer Night's Dream* when that guy Pyramid has to talk to his girlfriend through a crack in the wall?'

'You mean *Pyramus* and Thisbe,' I said.

'Yeah, that's him. Don't they try and kiss each other through the crack?'

'See you in a minute, George,' I said, nobly resisting the temptation to push my finger through the hole and poke him in the eye.

I went back to the garden just in time to see a triumphant Baby bearing an armful of stuff away into the house.

'Where's Auntie gone?' I asked. 'I think we might need some help here. There are about a hundred people outside waiting to charge in.'

'She's gone to get Dad and Uncle Jai,' Geena replied, looking slightly nervous as the noise outside began to swell.

'It's ten o'clock,' Jazz added. We all gazed at the gates, which were beginning to rock ever so slightly on their hinges. 'If we don't let them in soon, they're going to break in.'

Auntie hurried out with Dad and Uncle Jai, who immediately went over and stationed themselves one at each gate.

'Five – four – three – two – one!' Dad yelled, and then they swung the gates open.

There was a cheer. Then a mass of people poured in like locusts and split into three groups, one heading for Jazz's stall, one for Geena's and one for mine. I gulped and braced myself as a crowd swept towards me.

'Stop pushing!' Auntie yelled, materializing at my side like a helpful genie. Dad and Uncle Jai had already gone to Geena and Jazz's aid. 'And calm down or we'll throw you all out and the sale will be cancelled!'

There was a slight lull in the proceedings and I began taking money as fast as I could. My stall was stripped half bare in about ten minutes flat and I was kept so busy, even with Auntie's help, that I didn't have time to glance across at Geena and Jazz.

'Hi, Amber!' My mates Chelsea and Sharelle, flushed with victory and clutching their purchases, fought their way to the front of my table.

'I got *these* from Geena's stall,' Chelsea went on, waggling a pair of white and black trainers under my nose. 'Aren't they yours? They look like they've hardly been worn.'

'They haven't,' I said grimly. 'I didn't want to

sell those but Geena nicked them without my knowledge.'

'Oh dear.' Chelsea didn't look the slightest bit abashed. 'Well, tell you what, I'll wear them until your birthday and then I'll give them back to you. It will save me buying you a present.'

'How very kind,' I said.

An hour and a half later the sale was finally over. Cold, battered, bruised and exhausted, we dragged ourselves indoors and collapsed on the sofa to count our takings. We left Dad and Uncle Jai to clean up, and Auntie, who obviously felt sorry for us, offered to make hot chocolate and cheese on toast. Baby was nowhere to be seen. Presumably she was upstairs gloating over her designer bargains.

'One hundred and twenty pounds,' Jazz said. 'Beat that.'

'Eighty pounds,' Geena muttered.

'And I've got ninety-five,' I said. 'Jazz, you won. Well done.'

'Thanks, but I'm just too tired to celebrate at the moment.' Jazz yawned. 'I'll make sure to rub your noses in it later.'

'Just under three hundred pounds then.' Geena frowned. 'It's not much, is it? Not when our target's ten thousand.'

'There's plenty of time before Christmas,' I said brightly. 'We can carry on raising bits here and there, and once we get one BIG fund-raising idea, we'll be home and dry.'

Geena and Jazz didn't say a word. But I could tell from the looks on their faces that they didn't believe me.

Not surprising really, as I didn't even believe it myself.

Chapter Six

'All right,' I said, 'let's brainstorm some fund-raising ideas.'

I settled myself more comfortably on Geena's bed. I picked up my pen in a businesslike manner. I gazed expectantly at Geena and Jazz. And the result? Complete silence.

'Thank you for your input,' I said, throwing down my pen again in a sulk.

'Oh, come on, Amber,' Geena snapped. 'It's not quite that easy. I can think of lots of things like sponsored walks and all that, but there's only *three* of us. We're just not going to make very much money that way.'

'Geena's right,' said Jazz. 'We can't raise enough money doing normal sponsored events, so we need something different.' She eyed me speculatively. 'Why don't you shave your head, Amber?'

'Excuse me?'

'That's what people are always doing for Comic Relief and Children in Need,' Jazz replied. 'They get all their hair shaved off and people give them money.'

'I'd pay to see Amber get her head shaved,' said Geena. 'I think that's a cracking idea.'

'I am not getting my head shaved,' I said with emphasis. 'Anyway, why does it have to be me? Jazz has got the longest hair.'

'Forget it,' Jazz said quickly. 'It was just a joke.'

Geena was frowning thoughtfully. 'I was wondering if we couldn't set up some kind of dating agency at school,' she mused. 'You know, cut out all that stupid *my friend fancies your friend* type thing.'

'Is that how *you* got together with your boyfriend?' Jazz asked, smirking.

'I told you, I don't have a boyfriend,' Geena retorted angrily. 'So kindly stop going on about it.'

'Well, we would if we thought you were telling the truth,' I replied.

Geena looked quite uncomfortable. She's never been that great at telling fibs (unlike me), and I was definitely beginning to think that Jazz was right. That, at one time or another, Geena had been out on a secret date with a real, live *boy*. Amazing!

'A dating agency is a daft idea really,' Geena said quickly, looking far too eager to change the subject. 'It would probably take ages to organize.'

'And we'd get blamed when people split up,' Jazz pointed out.

'OK, well, maybe not a dating agency then, but what about charging people for makeovers?' I suggested. 'We could be the Trinny and Susannah of Coppergate School.'

'That's not a bad idea,' said Jazz. 'There are loads of kids who haven't got a clue when it comes to clothes, make-up and hair—'

'I know who *I'd* nominate,' I butted in. 'Commandant Gareth. He's the stereotype swot. Messy hair, glasses, biro-stained fingers and always looks like he's walked to school through a wind tunnel.'

'We could offer to make him look like David Beckham,' said Jazz. 'Now *there's* a challenge.'

Have you ever been thinking about something – or someone – and suddenly they appear, almost as if *you've* made it happen? I glanced idly out of the window and there, to my utter surprise, was Gareth Parker. He was a little way off, standing on the corner of our street.

'There he is,' I said, 'and he's got *binoculars*.'

Geena and Jazz stared at me as if I was completely raving.

'Gareth Parker,' I explained impatiently. 'He's staring at our house through binoculars.'

We all scrambled over to the window.

'Oh, don't be ridiculous,' said Geena, 'he's not looking at our house.'

'Well, what's he doing then?' asked Jazz.

'Probably bird-watching,' said Geena.

'Ha!' Jazz was triumphant. 'I knew it! He probably enjoys train-spotting as well.'

I threw open the window and leaned out. 'Gareth!' I called. 'Gareth Parker!'

Gareth jumped a metre in the air. He lowered the binoculars and stared belligerently at me.

'Why are you staring at our house?' I demanded.

'I am not staring at your house,' Gareth blustered. 'I was watching a wagtail in that tree over there.'

'I can't see any wagtails,' I said suspiciously. I don't *actually* know what a wagtail looks like, but all I could see was ordinary old sparrows anyway.

'Do you actually *know* what a wagtail looks like?' Gareth asked in a superior tone.

'No, because we're not boring swotty freaks

like you,' Jazz yelled. 'Gareth, how much would you pay for a makeover?'

'What?' Gareth looked confused.

'A makeover,' Jazz repeated impatiently. 'We could sort out your hair and clothes and find you a girlfriend. How about it?'

Gareth looked as horrified as if we'd offered to eat him alive. 'I can't think of anything worse,' he said. And he took off down the road at speed.

'He's *such* a weirdo,' Jazz remarked, closing the window. 'I bet he's never even kissed a girl. Ooh!' She let out a shriek of triumph. 'What about a kissing booth? We could sell kisses and raise money that way.'

'Yes, George Botley would be bankrupt in no time,' Geena said, smirking.

'Ha ha,' I muttered. 'How completely non-hilarious. I can't see Dad and Auntie going for *that.*'

The bedroom door opened.

'Time to go to Auntie's, girls,' said Dad. We'd all been invited to Sunday lunch except Baby, who'd gone to her friend's house. Supposedly. 'How are you getting on with your fund-raising ideas?'

'Not very well,' I replied with a sigh.

'You know, you only have to ask if you'd like me to donate a bit more—' Dad began.

'Ooh, yes please!' Jazz said.

'No, but thanks anyway, Dad.' I narrowed my eyes warningly at Jazz, who looked sullen. 'We really want to do this *ourselves*.'

I'd had so many things on my mind that I hadn't really thought any more about Auntie and Uncle Jai not getting on so well a few days ago. But now, as soon as we went over there, I could tell straight away that things weren't quite right. When two people have been arguing and they stop when you come into the room, you can kind of *tell* by the atmosphere, can't you? And boy, was there an atmosphere in their living room.

'Is everything OK?' I asked as we sat down at the table.

I knew it was a mistake the minute I said it. Auntie fixed me with a cool stare while Uncle Jai fiddled with his cutlery.

'What do you mean, Amber?' Auntie asked.

WARNING! WARNING! My brain was flashing danger signals all over the place.

'Oh – er – well – nothing . . .' My voice tailed away feebly.

'Good.' Auntie shoved a dish of roast potatoes into my hands. It was quite hot. I winced but bravely kept my mouth shut.

'I thought your yard sale went brilliantly

yesterday,' Uncle Jai said warmly. 'Well done, girls.'

'I see that boy was hanging around again,' Dad remarked, helping himself to roast chicken. 'What's his name – George Buttley?'

'You mean George Botley,' Auntie replied. 'The one who has a crush on Amber.'

Geena and Jazz giggled. I tried to keep cool but I could feel myself turning the colour of a very, very ripe tomato.

'I'm not encouraging him,' I muttered. 'He just seems to like me, that's all.'

'I agree, it is quite odd,' Auntie said with a teasing smile. She seemed to have forgiven me for what I said earlier. 'But the poor boy seems smitten.'

'Amber keeps giving him tasks to do,' bigmouth Jazz chimed in. 'That's why there were so many people at the sale yesterday. George Botley got them there.'

I wilted under the curious gaze of Dad, Auntie and Uncle Jai.

'Look, it's only to keep George off my back,' I said quickly. 'He keeps hassling me to go out with him.'

'Well, you're far too young for *that*.' Dad looked very stern. 'Do you want me to have a word with him?'

'Or me?' Auntie added.

'God, no!' I gasped. 'I mean – er – thank you, but I think I can handle George Botley.'

'Believe me, anything that keeps George Botley out of trouble is a good thing,' said Uncle Jai, winking at me. He's s-o-o-o nice.

'Well, tell George he can take you out on a date when you're sixteen,' Dad went on, 'and not a minute before.'

'Oh, the girls know the rules,' Auntie said. 'And I'm sure none of them would *dream* of breaking them. I'm right, aren't I, girls?'

'Yes, Auntie,' we said dutifully. But I couldn't stop myself sneaking a look at Geena. She was overplaying the dutiful, wide-eyed and innocent bit. Jazz was thinking the same thing because she kicked my ankle under the table. A bit too hard, as it happens.

After lunch there was a general outcry when Dad said, very apologetically, that he had to pop out to the office to do a couple of hours' work. I knew that his firm were working on this important project, but *still*. It *was* Sunday.

'You know, Dad was like this just after Mum died,' I said thoughtfully as we helped Auntie and Uncle Jai clear the table. 'Remember? He spent lots of time at work then.'

'What are you trying to say, Amber?' asked Auntie.

'Well, perhaps all this fund-raising for Mum is upsetting Dad,' I said hesitantly. 'Reminding him of what happened. Maybe this is my fault.'

Auntie put down the pile of dirty plates she was holding and slipped her arm around me.

'Amber, that's not the case at all. Your dad's very proud of what you're doing, all three of you.'

'Yes, he actually told us so,' Uncle Jai said gently. 'Look, he probably *is* just very busy at work. Simple as that.'

I nodded, although I wasn't entirely convinced. Auntie gave me a squeeze and then picked up the plates.

'Right, after we've loaded the dishwasher, let's have a drive out into the countryside,' she suggested. 'We can pick Baby up from her friend's house on the way.'

'But she's not expecting us till six,' Jazz pointed out.

'Exactly,' Auntie agreed cheerfully. 'So we'll find out where she *really* is and what she's been doing.'

'Great stuff!' Jazz said with glee.

As we went home to get our coats, I didn't say

much. It had suddenly struck me that there seemed to be a lot of secrets around at the moment. All right, maybe Dad *was* just busy at work, but there was definitely something going on with Auntie and Uncle Jai. Then there was Geena and her mysterious behaviour. Even if she didn't have a boyfriend *now*, my sisterly intuition had convinced me that she *had* been out with someone, sometime. And yet I was no closer to finding out the truth . . .

Honestly, all these mysteries are *so* bad for my health.

'Look, we *have* to decide on our next fund-raising idea,' I said with determination as we entered the school playground on Monday morning. The weekend had ended quite amusingly with Baby being caught red-handed with Rocky in the Spicy Samosa café on the Broadway when she should have been at her friend's house. Her subsequent sulks and tantrums had been even more entertaining than *Who's in the House?*

'Amber, you've been saying this very same thing for the last two days,' Geena replied. 'And we still haven't managed to come up with anything yet.'

'But we have to do something at least every

week or we haven't got a hope of raising that money by Christmas,' I pointed out.

'What about getting your heads shaved?' Kim suggested. 'I'd pay loads to see that.'

'Yes, it's not so bad,' added Kiran, who has very short cropped hair.

'We are *not* getting our heads shaved,' said Geena.

'Why don't we ask George Botley?' Jazz said with a smirk. 'He's done brilliantly with his tasks so far. He might have a few suggestions.'

'No, let's not bother George,' I said hastily, but Jazz was already screeching his name at the top of her lungs.

George came strolling across the playground towards us. 'Hi, wassup?'

'George, we need some fund-raising ideas and fast,' Jazz explained. 'Amber's too shy to ask you—'

'I am not!' I howled.

'So can *you* think of anything?' Jazz went on, ignoring me.

George looked thoughtful. 'You could sell kisses,' he suggested. 'I'd buy some.'

'No,' I interjected, 'we are not selling kisses. And we're not shaving our heads either,' I added, as I saw George eyeing Jazz's long locks speculatively.

'Shame.' George pondered for another minute. 'Well, what about a slave auction?'

'A slave auction?' Geena frowned. 'That's not a very PC term, is it?'

'What *is* a slave auction anyway?' asked Kim.

'Oh, the audience bid money for each slave and the winner gets the slave for a day's work,' Kiran explained. 'We had one at my old school. It was a laugh.'

'George, try to keep up,' I said patiently. 'There are only three of us. *Three* slaves. That means we're not going to be able to raise very much money.'

'I'd bid loads for you, Amber,' George replied with a rather scary wink. 'But why do there only have to be three of you?'

'Oh, well, let me see,' I said. 'One.' I pointed to myself. 'Two.' I pointed at Jazz. 'And three.' I nodded at Geena. 'See?'

George shrugged. 'You've all got loads of friends, haven't you?' he said. 'Why don't you get some of them to join in? You can make lots more money that way.'

I stared at him in confusion. I couldn't think of anything to say.

'George, you're a genius!' Jazz declared. 'I think I might give you a hug.'

'OK,' George agreed, a bit too readily for my liking.

'Stay where you are, Jasvinder,' I said sternly. 'George, we want to raise this money *ourselves*—'

'We *are* raising it ourselves,' Geena butted in. 'We'll be organizing everything, won't we? What a great idea. George, I might have to hug you too.'

'Stop with all the hugging,' I said irritably. 'We don't even know that our friends will *want* to join in.'

'I will,' said Kiran and Kim together, right on cue. George grinned at me.

'Well, all right,' I muttered. 'I suppose it is a good idea.' Good idea? It was a *great* idea. I just wish I'd thought of it myself.

Now that we had our idea, courtesy of George Botley, we swung immediately into action. We dashed off to see Mr Grimwade before the bell to get his permission, and we agreed between us that we would hold the auction in the school hall on Thursday at lunch time.

'A very good idea, girls,' Mr Grimwade boomed approvingly when we had outlined all our plans. 'You're setting a great example for all our other pupils. I'm sure your mum would be very proud of you. And I'll be coming along to bid for one of you, of course.'

'Great,' Geena said faintly. 'Thanks, sir.'

'Oh, I hope Grimwade doesn't bid for *me*,' I muttered as we left his office. 'Can you imagine? He'll have his slave cleaning the paintwork and picking up litter in the playground.'

'Don't be daft, Amber,' said Jazz with a smirk. 'There's only one person who's going to win *you*, and that's George Botley.'

'Yes, I wonder what your slave duties for George will involve, Amber?' Geena mused, also smirking quite annoyingly.

I gulped slightly. Still, if George was willing to bid a lot for me, we'd make more money that way. But if no one else bid, he might get me for ten pence. Scary thought.

'I've just realized that we need someone to run the auction and take the bids,' said Geena.

'What about Mr Hernandez?' I suggested. 'People would pay just to come and see him.' My form teacher was legendary throughout the school for his wacky dress sense and even wackier sense of humour.

'Ooh, brill idea alert!' Jazz exclaimed. 'Why don't all the slaves dress up? That would make it loads more fun.'

'Jazz, we don't have time to make costumes before Thursday—' I began.

'No, no, we'll borrow them from the drama studio,' Jazz interrupted eagerly.

'Good thinking, Jasvinder,' Geena approved.

As we scooted off down the corridor to see Ms Woods, the head of drama, I began to feel optimistic all over again. We were getting on with the business of raising money, and we still had four weeks or so until Mr Morgan's deadline. I was confident that I could still come up with one BIG fund-raising effort before then which would net us a whole heap of cash . . .

But by the time Thursday, the day of the slave auction, came round, I was feeling rather annoyed again. The only thing everyone was talking about at school that morning was *Who's in the House?* The night before there had been an unexpected mid-week eviction and Katy Simpson (who wasn't famous but was the ex-wife of someone who *was* famous) had got the boot. So now there were only three contestants left for the Grand Finale tomorrow – Luke Lee, Romy Turner and Molly Mahal.

'*Who's in the House?* has really stolen our limelight,' I complained as we wandered through the playground. 'Do you think anyone will even *remember* that there's a slave auction today?'

'Well, Mr Morgan will mention it again in assembly this morning,' Geena replied. 'And it's really cold today. So loads of kids will come to watch rather than freeze to death outside.'

'I'm still not sure exactly what I'm supposed to do,' Kim said nervously.

'Look, Kim, it's simple,' I said, for possibly the hundredth time. 'Someone comes along and bids for you and you have to do jobs for them.' We'd fixed on tomorrow, Friday, as the day when the slaves would perform their tasks for the winning bidders. 'Nobody's going to ask you to split the atom or do a bungee jump. It's just a bit of fun. That's all.'

Kim said nothing but didn't look convinced.

We'd managed to round up seventeen of our friends, including Kim and Kiran, who'd agreed to be slaves, so there were twenty of us in total. Mr Grimwade had arranged for us all to have lunch fifteen minutes early so that we could get into our costumes and be ready for the auction to start.

When we arrived at the canteen, Mrs Openshaw was on guard, waiting for us.

'Now, you haven't forgotten about getting me

Molly Mahal's autograph, have you, Amber?' she called as soon as she saw me.

'Of course not,' I replied, hoping I didn't look as guilty as I felt. I'd *completely* forgotten about it. 'I'll have to wait until *Who's in the House?* finishes though.'

'Oh, of course.' Mrs Openshaw winked at me and kindly gave me extra broccoli. Yum.

'I wonder if Molly's going to win,' said Chelsea as we all gathered round one of the large tables. 'What do you think?'

'Oh, I think she will,' Shweta, Jazz's friend, replied solemnly. 'She's so great, isn't she? Everyone loves her.'

'I think she's had cosmetic surgery since she was here, don't you?' Kyra, Geena's mate, chimed in. 'I reckon she's had her eyes done and—'

'Look, can we forget about *Who's in the House?* just for five minutes?' I snapped. 'I'd like to remind you that we have something equally important happening right here at Coppergate.'

'What's that then?' asked Sharelle. 'Oh, you mean the slave auction.'

'Yes, I do.' I glared at her. 'So can we keep our minds on that please?'

There was silence for about ten seconds, apart from the sound of chewing.

'I don't know,' Jazz said thoughtfully, 'I think Romy Turner's got a good chance, especially if she wears that silver bikini again.'

'What bikini?' Kiran scoffed. 'It's so tiny you'd need a magnifying glass to see it.'

They all started talking again and I sighed. I was getting quite sick of *Who's in the House?* Thank goodness the programme finished tomorrow. Maybe then people would concentrate on our fund-raising events.

Half an hour later we were all costumed up and waiting backstage in the school hall.

'There are lots of kids coming in,' Jazz reported with satisfaction as she peeped through the curtains. She was dressed as Pocahontas in what I personally thought was a rather too tight and too short tunic, along with a feather headdress. I was much more tasteful in a Spanish flamenco dress with my hair drawn back tightly into a bun. 'And teachers too,' Jazz went on. 'Oh!' she gave a yelp of surprise. 'Auntie's just come in with Uncle Jai.'

'I wonder what *she's* doing here?' Geena remarked. She had fought it out with Kyra for the flouncy, sequinned Fairy Godmother outfit, and was now swanning around backstage, waving her wand triumphantly. Kyra, meanwhile, was clanking about sulkily, dressed as the Tin Man from *The Wizard of Oz*.

'Are you ready, girls?' Mr Hernandez poked his head round the curtain. He was wearing a new purple shirt decorated with bright green lizards. 'If so, we'll make a start. Let's have you all out on the stage.'

'Sir, can you give me a hand?' Kim wailed, trying to hobble after the rest of us. She was dressed as a mermaid and her fishy tail was rather tight. 'I can't walk!'

Without further delay, Mr Hernandez made an executive decision and slung Kim over his shoulder in a fireman's lift. Then he carried her onto the stage and put her down. There were cheers and whoops from the audience.

'I'm sure that's against health and safety regulations,' I heard Mr Grimwade say pompously to Auntie and Uncle Jai as we followed Kim and Mr Hernandez out onto the stage. 'What if there's a fire? Kimberley won't be able to get out of the building fast enough.'

I was pleased (and relieved) to see that the hall was packed with kids and teachers. I was not at all pleased to see George Botley right at the very front of the stage, grinning up at me confidently. I'd asked George to be a slave himself but he'd refused, saying he was 'totally looking forward to being a bidder'. His words. Oh dear.

Mr Hernandez began banging maniacally on the lectern with an auctioneer's hammer. I have no idea where he got the hammer from but I could see Mr Grimwade wincing.

'Pray silence!' shouted Mr Hernandez. 'Today we have a super, a spiffing, a totally splendiferous auction for you. You, the audience' – he pointed the hammer at the crowd and the front row ducked nervously – 'will have the chance to bid for your very own slave in aid of the school library fund. So why waste any more time? Life is short and we're all getting older, so let's meet our first slave right away. The very lovely Jasvinder Dhillon!'

Jazz stepped forward from the line and there were a good few rather vulgar cheers as the boys clocked the length of her skirt (or lack of it).

'I'll start the bidding at one English pound,' Mr Hernandez declared. 'Any takers?'

'Five pounds,' Auntie called. Jazz, who was beaming all over her face and flicking her plaits flirtatiously, looked rather peeved.

'Ten pounds,' said Mr Grimwade, and Jazz looked even more worried.

The bidding crept up as a gaggle of boys who

all fancied Jazz joined in as well as some of her friends. Jazz had obviously ordered them to bid and then pull out at the last minute to make her look more popular. A truly despicable idea. I wish I'd thought of it.

The total stood at thirteen pounds seventy-five pence and was still going strong when a new bidder joined in.

'Fifteen pounds,' said Gareth Parker from the back of the room.

'No!' Jazz shrieked.

'What's he up to?' I whispered to Geena.

'Silence, please, slaves!' Mr Hernandez ordered imperiously. 'The bid stands at fifteen pounds.'

'Twenty pounds,' Mr Grimwade bellowed.

'Twenty-five,' said Auntie crisply.

'Twenty-six pounds,' Gareth added.

The other bidders had fallen away by now and Mr Grimwade shook his head too. Jazz stared beseechingly at Auntie.

'Thirty pounds,' Auntie offered.

Gareth hesitated, then shrugged and didn't say anything. Jazz heaved a loud sigh of relief.

'And the winner of our first slave is Mrs Arora,' Mr Hernandez announced as Auntie handed over the cash. 'Thank you. Now do make sure you work Jasvinder's fingers right down to the bone.'

'Oh, I intend to,' Auntie replied. 'I have a long list of chores that she *should* have done, going back months.'

Jazz looked extremely glum.

Things were going with a swing now. Next up was Kim, who tried to put a brave face on it when she was won for a bargain seventeen pounds twenty pence by Mr Grimwade. Mr Grimwade then announced that he was also there to bid on Mr Morgan's behalf because the headteacher needed someone to clean out the school's trophy cabinet. Kiran was the lucky slave there, going for twenty pounds.

'That sounds like a bum job,' I whispered to her. 'Sorry about that.'

Kiran shrugged. 'Oh, well, it's all for a good cause, isn't it?'

The auction went on, our friends going for amounts between five and twenty-five pounds. Most of them were won by teachers, but there was a minor sensation when Kyra Hollins was won by the boyfriend she'd dumped only two days previously.

'Do I *have* to?' she grumbled loudly after Christian Jones had apparently bid his life savings for her (thirty-one pounds fifty pence). 'It's not fair!'

'I can see why you're dressed as the Tin Man,' Christian announced soulfully, 'because you really don't have a heart.'

The mystery of Gareth Parker deepened even more when it was Geena's turn to be auctioned. As she stepped forward, he pushed his way to the front of the stage and stood there, arms folded, glowering at us.

'And now' – Mr Hernandez banged his hammer furiously – 'our next slave is the utterly fabulous Miss Geena Dhi—'

'Thirty pounds,' Gareth snarled.

Everyone turned to stare at him as Geena flushed pink with rage.

'He's up to something,' I said to Jazz. 'He's definitely up to something.'

'I agree,' said Jazz. 'But what?'

'That's a *very* high opening bid, Gareth,' Mr Hernandez said approvingly. 'Anyone else?'

'Er, excuse me.' Uncle Jai was clearing his throat apologetically. 'I'd like to bid, please. Thirty-five pounds.'

Geena beamed at him, only to scowl when Gareth snapped, 'Thirty-seven pounds.'

'Forty pounds,' said Uncle Jai.

Gareth looked defiant. 'Forty-one.'

'Forty-five.'

'I'm out,' Gareth muttered, slumping in defeat.

Geena waved jauntily across the room at Uncle Jai. 'Thanks,' she called.

'Don't mention it,' Uncle Jai called back. 'Your aunt asked me to bid. I think she has plans for you.'

'Yes, Geena, you haven't done half your chores either,' said Auntie. 'I have a full programme of activities planned for you tomorrow.'

'Oh, rats,' Geena muttered sulkily.

I smiled. I was extremely relieved that we'd decided that people were only allowed to win one slave each. But I was a little concerned that nobody would bid for me now except George Botley. I think George had had the same thought because he was looking ever so pleased with himself.

'And finally – our last slave!' Mr Hernandez boomed. 'The one, the only, the once-in-a-lifetime Miss Ambajit Dhillon!'

There were whoops and cheers, the loudest coming from George Botley, which was highly embarrassing.

'Any bids?' called Mr Hernandez.

George's hand shot into the air. 'Five pounds,' he offered.

Please, somebody, anybody else.

'Five pounds fifty pence.'

Gareth Parker again! I wasn't sure whether to be angry or relieved. George or Gareth? It was a terrible decision that no one should be forced to make.

A few other kids and teachers joined in, but George and Gareth continued to put the price up slowly and the others fell away. Gareth offered nineteen pounds, and for the first time George started looking a bit uncomfortable. He opened his mouth to speak but someone else got in before him.

'Twenty quid,' said Rocky from the back of the hall, not even bothering to remove his iPod headphones.

I let out a huge sigh of relief. Rocky probably only wanted to buy me to have someone to sit and listen to his extraordinarily bad rap music (taking the term 'captive audience' to a whole new level). But even that would be better than being at George or Gareth's beck and call for a day.

Gareth shook his head and stomped out of the hall. Ha! That was the end of *him* and his little game. Whatever that game might be.

George was looking worried too. 'Twenty-one,' he said hesitantly.

'Twenty-two.' Rocky didn't miss a beat.

George frowned up at Mr Hernandez. 'Twenty-two pounds and a bag of Walkers salt and vinegar.'

'George, you know my weakness for salt and vinegar crisps only too well,' Mr Hernandez said solemnly. 'But rules are rules. Hard cash only, I'm afraid.'

'Sorry,' George said apologetically, glancing up at me. 'I'm out.'

Thank goodness!

'I'll try to bear the pain, George,' I assured him.

'I now declare this auction over.' Mr Hernandez beat a final tattoo with his hammer on the lectern. 'And I'm pleased to tell you that the girls have raised just over three hundred pounds!'

There was a round of loud applause and then everyone began filing out for afternoon lessons.

'Thanks for bidding for me, Rocky,' I said as he climbed onto the stage to pay Mr Hernandez. 'You saved my life.'

'What?' Rocky was texting away on his mobile. 'Oh, I wasn't bidding for myself. Baby asked me to bid for her.'

'*What!*' I screamed.

'Yes, I'm just texting her now to tell her I won.' Rocky sent the text and scowled. 'She'd better pay me back for this as well. She owes me a ton of cash as it is.'

Horror-struck, I tottered backstage to join the others.

'Poor George,' Jazz remarked, removing her feather headdress. 'I did feel sorry for him when he missed out on Amber.'

'Never mind George, what about you and me?' Geena demanded. 'Auntie's going to have us doing chores before and after school tomorrow. She'll want to get her money's worth all right.'

'Well, if you want to know something even more tragic,' I said glumly, 'Rocky was bidding on Baby's behalf.'

I'd like to say that Geena and Jazz were sympathetic, but they just roared with laughter.

As we went home after school that evening, quite a few people came up to me and said how much they'd enjoyed the slave auction. But, as usual, most of the playground talk was about that night's edition of *Who's in the House?* Would someone else be kicked out before the Grand Finale tomorrow night? Would Molly Mahal take glory, or would Romy Turner's string bikinis win the day? Even Luke Lee had an outside chance, what with his ageing eighties fan base.

I was so annoyed with the programme taking

away most of the attention from our fund-raising efforts that I almost decided not to watch tonight. Note: I did say *almost* decided. Well, these things hook you like a fish and you *have* to watch, don't you? It's a bit like picking at a scab. You know it's bad for you, but you just can't stop yourself.

'Look!' I groaned as we reached our house. Baby was sitting in the window like a shark waiting for her next victim to chance along the way. That would be me, then.

'What's she holding?' asked Jazz as we walked towards the front door.

'Two sheets of A4 paper,' I sighed, 'which I'm betting is my list of jobs for tomorrow.'

Baby spotted us outside and began grinning like a loon through the window.

'Bad luck, Amber,' Geena chuckled as we went in. 'I bet even Auntie hasn't got *that* much planned for me and Jazz.'

'How wrong can you be?' Auntie appeared in the living room doorway and thrust one list at Geena and another at Jazz. 'There are two pages each, by the way. Baby and I printed them all out on the computer.'

'This is inhuman,' Jazz wailed, scanning the sheets. 'Even slaves have rights.'

'Hi, Amber.' A grinning Baby handed me her

list over Auntie's shoulder. 'I'd like all these things done tomorrow, please. You'll probably have to get up an hour or two earlier, but no pressure.'

'I'm going to garrotte George Botley for suggesting that stupid slave auction,' I muttered.

'Anyway, on a lighter note, I have some interesting news for you,' Auntie went on. 'When I got home after the slave auction this afternoon, someone rang me from the local TV news programme.'

'You mean they'd heard about the slave auction and wanted to put it on the local news?' I asked, perking up.

'I'm afraid not,' Auntie replied. 'They want to come and film us watching *Who's in the House?* tomorrow night. Everyone knows Molly stayed with us quite recently and they think it would be interesting to film our celebrations if she wins tomorrow.'

'Oh.' Sure, it would be a bit of a laugh to be on the TV. But all this *Who's in the House?* frenzy was seriously beginning to get on my nerves.

'Ooh! I'm going to be on TV!' Baby squealed. 'Out of my way, losers.' She barged past me, Geena and Jazz, and charged upstairs. 'I've got to plan my outfit.'

'Baby, they're only going to film us for a very brief period,' Auntie called after her, 'and I'm sure they won't show the clip at all if Molly doesn't win.'

But Baby had gone, dreaming of TV stardom.

'She's such a clunkhead,' Geena said dismissively. 'I mean, it's only the local news, for goodness' sake. Nothing special. Do you think I'll have time to go to the hairdresser's after school?'

'No,' said Auntie. 'You have slave duties to perform.'

Geena scowled.

'*Are* we going to celebrate if Molly wins?' asked Jazz. 'I wasn't planning to throw a party or anything.'

'I think the news people are hoping we'll jump up and down and cheer loudly,' Auntie replied. 'They said they wanted the same atmosphere as you find in a pub when the England football team are playing.'

'What, doom and gloom, and people drowning their sorrows in drink?' I asked.

Auntie smiled. 'I think they meant jumping around and cheering when England score a goal. Oh, and they want us to invite as many people who knew Molly as possible to come along.'

'All right,' I agreed absently. An idea had just occurred to me and I took it up and looked at it from all angles, while Geena and Jazz started discussing what outfits they were going to wear tomorrow.

The news crew were coming to film us because we knew Molly Mahal, and because of the popularity of *Who's in the House?* of course. But appearing on TV, even just the local news, could be great publicity, in some way, for our own fund-raising efforts.

How exactly?

I just had to figure that one out before tomorrow night.

Chapter Seven

'And the Oscar for Best Actress goes to . . . Amber Dhillon!'

Blushing and smiling, I gathered up the long sparkly skirts of my expensive crimson dress and sashayed my way over to the stage, diamonds twinkling in the flashing lights of the cameras. The applause was deafening. People were whooping and cheering, and it was all for me.

'Go, Amber!'

'Amber, you're the greatest!'

'We love you, Amber!'

'Oi, Amber! Wake up, you lazy lump!'

'Huh?' I groped my way out of a deep sleep, leaving my delicious dream far behind me. I opened one eye cautiously. Baby was looming over me in the early-morning greyness.

'Oh, good, you're awake,' she said, strolling

over to the door. 'Hurry up, there's loads to do.'

'What time is it?' I called feebly after her.

'Six a.m.' Baby didn't even bother to hide the smugness in her voice. 'You'd better get on with my list of jobs, or I'll want my money back.'

'Wassgoinon?' Geena emerged from under the duvet, yawning, her hair sticking up like porcupine spikes. She clocked Baby by the door and grinned sleepily at me. 'Bye, Amber. Have fun.'

'Don't get *too* comfy, Geena,' said Baby as Geena curled up again. 'Auntie's waiting for you and Jazz downstairs.'

'What!' Geena howled, sitting bolt upright. 'This is contravening my human rights!'

Baby shrugged. 'Whatever,' she said, and went out.

Geena and I dragged ourselves out of bed. I didn't know it was possible to sleep standing up, but Geena fell asleep buttoning her school shirt. I poked her awake and we wandered, gummy-eyed and yawning, out onto the landing, where we bumped into Jazz. She was slumped over the banisters, snoring loudly.

Geena slapped her on the back.

'I wasn't asleep,' Jazz mumbled, eyes still closed.

I left the two of them to help each other

downstairs, a step at a time, and stumbled into Baby's room.

'At last!' Baby said, rolling her eyes theatrically. 'Right, my washing's over there. You can take that downstairs and load it into the machine first of all. Then you can make the bed. You can tidy and clean out my make-up bag. Oh, and clean all my shoes and boots as well. You're lucky, I only brought fifteen pairs with me . . . AMBER!'

Baby's voice seemed to be coming from a very long way away.

'Are you asleep?' she demanded.

'No.' I propped my eyelids open with my fingers. 'I heard you. Washing first.'

I gathered up an armful of T-shirts and jeans and trudged downstairs. Geena was emptying the kitchen bin and Jazz was cleaning the top of the cooker. Auntie, meanwhile, was making coffee. She looked as fresh as a daisy.

'This will keep you going,' she remarked, handing me a cup.

I sipped the coffee as I plodded back upstairs, yawning. But it actually wasn't the coffee that woke me up. As I reached the top of the stairs, I could hear Baby talking on her mobile. She sounded agitated.

'I *know* I said to ring me early, but this

morning's not a good time,' she was muttering. 'Everyone else is awake too, and I don't want them to find out what's going on.'

Uh-oh! Instantly I was as alert and awake as if I'd drunk a hundred cups of coffee. Something was going on! I froze on the top step, straining to hear what Baby said next.

'Well, has anything changed?' she asked urgently. There was silence for a few minutes. 'No! You *can't* be serious!' she gasped. 'What's going to happen now? What are we going to do?'

'Get out of my way, Amber.' Jazz's voice behind me made me almost jump out of my skin. She was trudging wearily up the stairs towards me. 'Auntie says I have to change my bed and if I don't keep moving, I might just fall down and die of exhaustion.'

Baby must have heard Jazz too because by the time I went into her room, she'd rung off and her phone was lying on the bed.

'About time too,' she snapped with a nasty glare. 'Here.' She thrust a make-up bag the size of a small suitcase at me. 'Give this a good clean. I'm going for a shower.'

This was a foul mood, even for Baby, who wasn't known for being Miss Sweetness and Light. I was *definitely* intrigued. Another mystery to add to the others ... Honestly, the TV people should make a documentary about my family and their secrets. It'd be a lot more interesting than *Who's in the House?*

I told Geena and Jazz what I'd overheard on the way to school that morning. As all three of us were having trouble keeping our eyes open after two hours of hard labour, talking it over helped to keep us awake.

'Maybe Baby was speaking to Rocky,' Jazz suggested with an almighty yawn.

'But why would she tell him to ring her so early?' I asked. 'It doesn't seem to fit.'

Suddenly my own phone bleeped twice. I fished it out of my pocket and saw a number I didn't recognize.

HI A, CAN I CUM RD 2 YRS 2NITE 4 THE W.I.T.H. FILMING. GEORGE XXX

I stared at the screen in disbelief. We'd texted and called some friends yesterday evening to invite them to the filming, but George Botley was not one of them.

'*George Botley* has my mobile number?' I roared. 'How – what – who?'

I homed straight in on Jazz, who was looking ever so slightly sheepish.

'Yes, it was me,' she admitted.

'Oh, how amusing,' Geena said with glee.

'Jazz, you *know* the rules,' I said savagely. 'George Botley does *not* get my mobile number. Ever. I don't want the trauma of knowing that Dad or Auntie can pick up my phone and see a message from George which *might* be incriminating.'

'Oh, chill out and stop using long words.' Jazz yawned again. 'I only gave him the number yesterday, and he donated some money to our Mum Fund in return.'

'How much?' I demanded.

'Three quid,' Jazz replied.

'Oh, great,' I said. 'My privacy and peace of mind have been sold down the river for *three pounds*. How reassuring.'

'It's three pounds more than we had before,' Jazz replied, looking not one whit ashamed of herself. 'Why *don't* we let George come? The more the merrier – *and* we can pass round a collecting tin tonight too. Those TV people should be good for a few quid.'

'Great idea, Jazz,' Geena approved.

Jazz whisked my phone out of my hand and began texting a reply to George. I made a feeble attempt to stop her but I was really too tired to fight it out. At that moment we were joined by Kim and Kiran, who both looked rather glum. Seeing as Kim was Mr Grimwade's slave for the day and Kiran was cleaning out the trophy cabinet for Mr Morgan, I could hardly blame them.

'Sure you won't change your mind and come along tonight?' I asked Kiran.

She shook her head. 'Thanks, but I came to the school after Molly Mahal was here so I never met her. Anyway, my mum's working this evening so I have to look after the kids.'

'I can't wait,' Kim chimed in. 'How many people will be there?'

'About twenty,' Geena replied.

'And George Botley, apparently,' I said bitterly. I was feeling grumpy, I admit, because I still hadn't come up with a plan to exploit the potential of our TV appearance. Maybe the news people would let me ask for donations to our Mum Fund on air. On the other hand, if Molly Mahal didn't win *Who's in the House?* we might not even make it onto the TV. The only other alternative was to ask Dad for more cash. I really didn't want to do that.

And there, in front of me, right under my nose as we walked into the school playground, was another of the mysteries that were driving me up the wall at the moment. Gareth Parker and his merry band of interfering nosy parkers (the sixth-formers) were buzzing busily around the playground again, annoying quiet, law-abiding pupils with their nonsense.

'So why *did* Gareth bid for us at the auction?' I mused aloud, watching him zoom over to chastise Darren Plummer for not tucking in his shirt.

'Oh, I would have thought that was obvious.' Geena shrugged. 'To wind us up.'

'Quite an expensive wind-up if he'd happened to win the bids though,' Jazz remarked.

'I'm going to ask him,' I decided, and marched over without further delay.

Gareth was lecturing Darren about his shirt, and Darren wasn't taking it lying down. Good for him. Although his counter-argument might have been more effective if he hadn't used *quite* so many swearwords. I tapped Gareth on the shoulder, quite hard actually, and he spun round. Darren, meanwhile, sloped off to join in a football game, leaving his shirt still hanging defiantly out.

'Good morning, Gareth,' I said briskly. 'I'd like to know why you bid for me and my sisters at the auction yesterday.'

Gareth immediately turned the colour of a

beetroot. 'Why not?' he snapped. 'It's a free country, isn't it?'

'Well, apparently not here at Coppergate School,' Geena retorted, staring pointedly round at the sixth-formers on patrol.

'Maybe he fancies us,' Jazz said, a wicked glint in her eye.

Gareth snorted derisively. 'As a matter of fact, *if* any of my bids had been successful, I was going to make you patrol the playground in the mornings with me and see how difficult the sixth-formers' job is. Oh, and get you collecting litter. Useful things like that.'

'I don't believe you,' I said. I was *sure* there was something else going on. But I didn't know what.

'That is entirely up to you, Amber,' Gareth said pompously, and strode off with dignity. Unfortunately, Darren Plummer now decided to take his revenge by belting the football straight at the back of Gareth's knees.

'Sorry,' Darren called, smirking, as Gareth buckled and almost fell. 'Accident.'

I couldn't help smirking myself until George Botley sidled up to me out of nowhere.

'Hey, Amber.' He winked at me. 'Thanks for the cute text.'

How appalling.

'Jazz!' I hissed. 'What did you put in that text you sent George?'

But Jazz had already taken off into school, laughing her daft head off.

I'd always wondered how people managed before mobile phones were invented. However, after today, I was beginning to think that one could have too much of a good thing. Firstly I had to make it clear to George Botley that the loved-up text message with lots of kisses and hearts had been sent by Jazz and not by me. Then, of course, there was the mysterious conversation I'd heard Baby having earlier. And this was followed, at lunch time, by yet more mobile melodrama.

'Don't try to get away from me, Jazz,' I panted, pursuing her down the corridor. 'I read that text you sent to George and you're going to have to pay.'

'You've got no sense of humour, Amber,' Jazz grumbled, dodging swiftly round the corner and outside into the playground. 'That's your trouble.'

'I've decided on our next fund-raising event,' I replied, still following. 'We're shaving your head.'

'Ooh!' Jazz came to a full stop and I almost fell right over her. 'What's Geena doing?'

Geena was tucked away in a quiet corner of the playground, talking on her mobile. Her face was red and she was waving her free hand around a lot.

'She's arguing with someone,' Jazz said gleefully. 'But who?'

'Silence,' I ordered, putting my finger to my lips. 'Follow me.'

We edged our way across the playground towards Geena. However, we could probably have charged towards her in a Sherman tank and she wouldn't have noticed. She was totally intent on her call.

'Look, there's no point to any of this,' she was saying. 'I've made my decision and it's over. End of story.'

Looking excited, Jazz gave me a great nudge in the ribs. I wasn't expecting it and overbalanced, toppling slowly sideways, right into Geena's eyeline.

'Yes?' Geena enquired coldly, stabbing immediately at the off button on her phone. 'Is there something I can do for you?'

'Tell us who you were talking to,' said Jazz.

'It was private,' Geena replied.

'Well, we guessed as much,' I said. 'That's *exactly* why we want to know.'

'Were you talking to your boyfriend?' Jazz demanded.

'I'm fed up with these stupid questions,' Geena snapped. 'I *do not* have a boyfriend, but I *am* allowed to have some sort of life away from you two, you know.'

'Wherever did you get *that* ridiculous idea from?' I asked.

'And I don't think Dad and Auntie would agree,' Jazz added.

Geena opened and closed her mouth but couldn't think of anything to say. Shoving her phone into her bag, she flounced off.

'Ooh, I'd like to get a look at that phone,' Jazz said with longing.

'Forget it, she'll delete everything,' I replied. 'But we're on her case and we just need to keep our eyes and ears open. Sooner or later we'll find out what's going on, or Geena will crack and tell us. One or the other.'

'She'll crack,' Jazz said confidently. 'No one can resist my constant wind-ups if I *really* put my mind to it.'

'Go, Jasvinder,' I said with approval.

It's good to talk. Apparently. But I definitely began to question the truth behind this statement later that day. We rushed out of school as soon as the bell rang, eager to get home and prepare for the arrival of the local news crew. I was fully expecting a fist-fight to get into the bathroom first, but I'd forgotten that we were still on slave duty until 5.30, our official clocking-off time. Auntie spied us from next door as we elbowed each other to get through the gate and pushed and shoved our way up the garden path.

'Hello, girls,' she called, opening the window. 'Geena and Jazz, I'll be round at five thirty exactly to check that you've finished your lists of jobs.'

Geena and Jazz both muttered curses very quietly. I chuckled.

'Baby's gone to the hairdresser's,' Auntie went on. 'She expects her list to be finished too, Amber. Or she wants her money back.'

'Oh, blast it,' I muttered as Geena and Jazz sniggered.

Baby's list seemed longer than I remembered. I was *sure* she'd added a few more jobs to it when I wasn't looking. Sullenly I whizzed through them as fast as I could until I came to the last one. *Clean my bedroom.* OK, so I would push the vacuum cleaner around the room for a few minutes and that would be it. Downstairs I could hear Geena and Jazz arguing about kitchen cleaners like two housewives in a TV ad. It was still only quarter to five so they'd have to wait for Auntie to come over and OK their work. So, with any luck, I'd make it into the bathroom first and get to beautify myself before the news crew arrived, ha ha!

The front door slammed as I went out onto the landing. Was that Baby returning from the hair-dresser's? This could ruin all my carefully laid plans. I jumped forward and peered over the banister, only to see the top of Dad's head. Of course, he'd come home early from work to take part in the filming.

'I don't think that's going to be possible. It would be quite difficult at the moment.'

For a minute I thought Dad was talking to me. I could only just hear him though, because his voice was very low. *Then* I realized he was on his mobile.

'Thanks very much but I can't,' he went on. 'Really. Maybe some other time. No, I can't talk right now.'

Another mysterious mobile moment! Well, maybe I was exaggerating just a teeny-weeny bit. It was more the way Dad was acting. He looked so *secretive*, standing there in the hall, shoulders hunched over and speaking in such a low voice. And he kept casting anxious glances at the kitchen, where Geena and Jazz were still arguing.

'Dad!' Jazz bellowed, charging into the hall. 'Geena's hogging the Cillit Bang and won't let me have a spray!'

Dad was so unnerved, he fumbled to switch off his phone and dropped it instead. It clattered to the wooden floor and came apart.

'Geena, let your sister use the Silly Bang!' he called, scrabbling around on his hands and knees to retrieve the bits.

'*Cillit* Bang, Dad,' Jazz informed him. 'You know, *Bang and the dirt is gone!*'

'Er – right,' said Dad, looking completely flustered. Clutching the bits of his phone to his chest, he bolted into the study and closed the door.

I frowned. Was I the only sane and sensible person around here? The only one who could see really weird things going on all over the place? Or was I just making up mysteries where none existed?

Feeling a bit unsettled by it all, I abandoned Baby's list and went to find someone I could talk to.

'This is a surprise,' said Auntie as she let me in next door. 'I thought you'd be locked in the bathroom by now, getting ready for tonight.'

'I just thought I'd come over and say hello.' I wandered into the living room, where a pile of brightly coloured brochures on the coffee table caught my eye. I picked one up. '*Discover Australia and New Zealand,*' I read out. 'Are you and Uncle Jai going on holiday?'

'Well, we haven't had a proper honeymoon yet,' Auntie replied. 'I know we went away at half-term but that was only for a few days.'

'Australia's a long way away,' I remarked, flipping idly through the pages. It looked beautiful, though.

'Nine or ten thousand miles, actually.' Auntie scooped up the brochures and put them away in the magazine rack. 'What's the matter, Amber?'

'Oh.' Now that I was here, I didn't exactly know *why* I was here. Sure, there were lots of things I *thought* were going on but I couldn't mention some of them to Auntie. I couldn't ask her if she and Uncle Jai were getting along better now (I did not have a death wish), although maybe they were, as they were planning their honeymoon. And I didn't want to drop Geena in it. Not without proof, anyway!

'Um,' I said. 'Ah.'

'You'll have to give me a bit more of a clue than that,' said Auntie.

'Well . . . is Dad all right?'

'Amber, you asked me this before,' Auntie replied patiently. 'As far as I know – and although this may seem astounding to you, I don't know *everything* – your dad is fine. Fit and well and enjoying life.'

'He seems a bit on edge,' I said cautiously. I didn't want Auntie to know that I'd been listening to Dad's private conversations.

'You know what your trouble is, Amber,' said Auntie. 'You're a little too nosy for your own good.'

What a cheek! I was speechless. This coming from the maharani of all the interfering Indian aunties in the known world!

'You need to chill out and give people some space,' Auntie went on. 'Things will work themselves out one way or another.'

'OK,' I spluttered. 'Thanks for the advice.'

'You're welcome,' Auntie replied, looking not one bit embarrassed. Can you *believe* it?

When I got back home, there was a full-on row between Geena, Jazz and Baby about who was going to use the bathroom first. Auntie heard all the noise and came round to see what was going on. She decided to draw names out of a hat to prevent violence, and Baby, who had returned from the hairdresser's with a startling up-do of cascading curls, won. I, of course, was last.

By the time I'd showered and dressed in my chosen outfit (a bright red TopShop dress and long boots – very classy), the news crew had already arrived. I dashed downstairs as fast as my kitten heels could carry me and found three people – two men and a woman – rearranging our living room. Geena and Jazz were hovering around, both of them wearing new outfits, and Baby was standing in the middle of the room, smiling dazzlingly at the news crew whenever any of them caught her eye. She looked completely over the top in her black and white zebra-print mini-dress, leggings, high heels and a kilo of (real) gold jewellery. Auntie, Uncle Jai and Dad were there too, supervising the rearranging of the chairs.

'Is that it?' I said to Geena, feeling a little disappointed. 'Just the three of them and one camera?' I'd expected a bit more, to be honest. Lots of lights, cameras and action. OK, they'd brought a *few* lights with them but nothing much.

'We'll have the three girls sitting at the front,' said the woman, Martha Rigby, who appeared to be in charge. She turned to Baby. 'Are you one of the sisters who knew Molly Mahal?' she asked.

'Oh, yes,' Baby lied through her teeth. 'Shall I sit here?' And she plonked herself on a chair in the middle of the front row.

'Baby's staying with us at the moment, but I

think Geena, Amber and Jazz are the girls you mean,' said Auntie, skilfully ushering a sulky Baby from her chair and propelling us forward.

So we were going to be centre stage. This was *great*. Quick, Amber, think of some way you could exploit this fantastic opportunity to raise more money for the Mum Fund! But sadly, my mind remained a beautiful blank. We'd got some boxes ready to take a collection, but nothing else.

Things started to get rather more exciting when everyone else started to arrive. No prizes for guessing who was first to turn up.

'Hey, Amber.' George Botley dropped a couple of pound coins into the collecting box that Jazz waved under his nose and zoomed straight over to me. 'Can I sit next to you?'

'Sorry, George,' I said quickly. 'Immediate family only in the front row.'

'We could pretend I'm your fiancé,' George replied with a wolfish grin.

'And give my dad a heart attack live on camera?' I retorted. 'I think not.'

'Well, this is all very exciting!' Mrs Dhaliwal bustled in, elbowing George Botley aside without ceremony. Behind her was Mr Attwal from the local minimarket. Mrs Dhaliwal's a local busybody – not *quite* in the same league as Auntie, but not far behind. She also arranges marriages for anyone single she can get her hands on. 'I hope dear Miss Mahal is going to win, and not that frightful half-naked girl.'

'Oh, you mean Romy Turner,' said Mr Attwal. 'Yes, not a nice girl at all. I wonder if she'll wear that silver bikini tonight.'

I watched as Mrs Dhaliwal immediately went and sat right at the front. Baby, who'd reluctantly moved to the second row, began complaining loudly, and one of the news crew had to rush and sort it out.

I turned to Kim, who'd just arrived. 'Have you had your hair done?' I asked, looking her over suspiciously.

'Of course,' Kim said assertively. 'Why haven't you?'

I scowled. I'd barely had time to wash and dry it after being last into the shower.

Kim took off her coat and I raised my eyebrows. She was wearing one of the T-shirts that Molly Mahal had got printed to publicize the school's Bollywood party. It had a large photo of Molly's face on the front.

'What are you wearing *that* for?' I snorted.

'To show Molly a bit of support,' Kim replied. 'And I'm not the only one either.'

148

I glanced round. Chelsea, Sharelle and Geena and Jazz's mates had already arrived, and now that they'd taken their coats off, I could see that a fair few of them were also wearing the T-shirts. Chelsea and Sharelle had even cut off the bottoms of theirs (the out-of-date bit about meeting Molly at the party) so that they were showing off their bare midriffs.

'How stylish,' I said with heavy sarcasm.

'Wow, these T-shirts are *super*.' Martha hurried over, staring admiringly at Kim. She glanced at me. 'Do you girls have these?'

'Well . . . er – yes . . .' Fool! Why didn't I lie?

'Thanks a lot, Amber,' Geena said bitterly as she, Jazz and I trailed upstairs to fulfil Martha's orders and change out of our über-stylish outfits into Molly T-shirts and jeans.

By the time we got downstairs again, though, we cheered up a good deal. The atmosphere was getting quite lively and people were enjoying themselves. The news crew spent about half an hour telling us all *very* seriously to jump up and down and scream a lot if Molly Mahal won. They even made us rehearse a few times, which was rather embarrassing. I could tell that things were going to go *very* flat if Molly actually lost. Still, Dad had promised takeaways all round from the

Tip-Top Tandoori after the programme, so the evening wouldn't be a total loss.

To my surprise, Mr Grimwade had turned up, also wearing his too tight and too short Molly T-shirt. Rocky was also there, sitting with Baby. He hadn't actually met Molly as he'd only started at Coppergate this term, but I suppose the lure of being on TV was just too strong for a would-be rap superstar.

'I've written a special rap for Molly, if she wins,' Rocky said loudly. 'Do you think that lot will film me doing it?'

'I shouldn't think so for a moment,' Auntie said repressively. Rocky scowled, but he brightened again when Martha announced that they would be interviewing some of us after the winner of the programme was announced.

We were all really quite excited by the time *Who's in the House?* actually started.

'*And now – it's the moment you've all been waiting for!*' Kieron King said breathlessly. '*Tonight we're all going to find out who is this year's celebrity winner of WHO'S IN THE HOUSE?*'

Everyone standing around him went wild – you'd have thought he'd just announced that he'd found a solution to global warming. There were quite a few cheers in our living room as well.

'Oh, here we go,' Jazz grumbled as a long, long sequence of clips from the previous week's programmes began. 'This is going to take *hours*. Why can't they just tell us the winner and have done with it?'

'Because that would only take about five minutes,' I replied, 'and they want thousands of people to phone in so they can make loads of money.'

The numbers to vote for the three remaining contestants were being flashed up on the screen right now. Everyone in the room had their mobiles in their hands, including the news crew, and there were loud cheers as Molly's number came up. Then silence except for the sound of twenty-three people texting their vote. All right, I admit I'd decided to vote for Molly. She deserved it for the best acting role she'd ever played in her life – pretending to be a completely sweet, kind and lovely person.

'Ooh, you pig!' Baby screeched, trying to grab Rocky's phone. 'You're voting for Romy Turner!'

'So?' Rocky continued to text away, fending Baby off with his arm. 'She's hot. Anyway, *you* voted for Luke Lee.'

'I hope *some* of you are voting for Molly Mahal,' Martha remarked slightly disapprovingly.

Excitement was mounting as various other 'celebrities' – some of whom I'd never heard of, so how did that make them celebrities? – were interviewed and told us who they thought should win. The last part of the programme was individual interviews with each of the three remaining contestants – Molly, Romy and Lee. They each talked about what they had learned about themselves living in the house for ten weeks and what they'd do when they got out. Once again Molly came across as a naturally lovely and genuine woman with a sunny personality. I didn't see how she could lose – although I was sure Romy Turner's white dress with the plunging halter neck had won her many votes.

Finally the three contestants gathered at the door of the house to hear the verdict.

'At last!' Jazz shrieked as Kieron King waved the golden envelope tantalizingly in front of our noses. 'The suspense is killing me!'

'Get ready, everyone,' Martha Rigby warned as Kieron ripped open the envelope with a great flourish.

I don't know about the others but I barely registered what she said. Somehow, even though I *knew* this programme was manufactured rubbish, I'd got caught up in it. I'd got involved. I really was thrilled and excited to fever pitch, and I wanted Molly to win.

'The celebrity winner ... of WHO'S IN THE HOUSE? is ...' Kieron King was deliberately and cruelly drawing out the moment. I was on the edge of my seat and so was everyone else. 'MOLLY MAHAL!'

Our living room erupted like an overheating volcano. There were screams and cheers and applause, and I think every single person in the room was jumping up and down, making the floor shake. We were all genuinely thrilled.

'She did it!' Geena gasped.

'I knew she would!' Jazz added.

I was so busy celebrating along with everyone else that I'd completely forgotten about the film crew. Until a microphone was suddenly shoved right under my nose.

'Amber, we've just seen Molly Mahal announced as the winner of Who's in the House?,' Martha said briskly. 'You're obviously pleased?'

I blinked a bit, then remembered that they had told us they were going to do a few interviews. The noise in the room had quietened down slightly now and I heard Kieron King proclaim that Molly Mahal had polled over one hundred thousand votes from viewers to win. The programme had been *so* popular. It must have made *thousands* of pounds for the TV company . . .

And that was when a bold, a brave, a most *audacious* fund-raising idea popped into my head.

'Of course I'm thrilled!' I said, smiling widely. 'Big congratulations to Molly. But I'm even more pleased because Coppergate School is going to be holding its very own *Who's in the House?* contest during the next few weeks. Or should that be *Who's in the School?*!' I laughed brightly.

Martha was looking very interested. 'Really?' she asked eagerly.

I nodded. The TV was still blaring out, but in the rest of the room you could have heard a pin drop.

'My two sisters and I are raising money to have the Coppergate School library named after our mum. And just like *Who's in the House?*, ten contestants, including myself and my sisters, will be locked up inside Coppergate School!' I declared.

I glanced at Geena and Jazz. They were goggle-eyed.

'And just like *Who's in the House?*' – I paused dramatically – 'there can only be one winner!'

Chapter Eight

There was a stunned silence which lasted for about four seconds.

So, thinking on my feet, I quickly added, 'If Mr Morgan, our headteacher, agrees, of course.'

Then – uproar.

'Cut! *Cut!*' Mr Grimwade bellowed, bouncing to the front of the room and waving his arms around like a demented movie director. 'I insist that you stop filming! Mr Morgan will certainly *not* approve of this so-called fund-raising event!'

My knees sagged and I felt slightly sick as Mr Grimwade launched into a full-scale argument with the news crew. Everyone else in the room seemed to be yelling their heads off too. But I also felt exhilarated. I was convinced that at last I'd found the really *huge* fund-raising event we'd been looking for.

'Amber, are you insane?' Geena yelled in my ear, looking quite disapproving.

'She's finally flipped,' Kim said, also frowning. 'I always knew it was going to happen some day.'

'I just can't see how this would work.' Jazz eyed me thoughtfully. 'But it's actually not a bad idea.'

'Thanks, Jazz,' I said, grateful for some support, however tiny.

'Don't thank me.' Jazz shrugged. 'It's Dad, Auntie and Uncle Jai you have to convince.'

I turned slightly to see Dad, Auntie and Uncle Jai staring very sternly at me. I smiled tentatively at them, but did not get a flicker in return.

Mr Grimwade was still arguing heatedly with the news crew. 'I demand that you cut that part of the film out!' he blustered.

'Who are you, then?' Martha asked coolly, signalling to the crew to pack their equipment away.

'I am the deputy head at Coppergate School, and I am speaking on behalf of the headteacher, Mr Morgan,' Mr Grimwade replied pompously.

Martha looked unimpressed. 'Well, get Mr Morgan to ring me at the studios, and we can discuss this,' she replied, and turned away.

Mr Grimwade scowled and directed a fierce look at me that made me gulp.

'I think it's a great idea, Amber,' George Botley called from the back row. 'Go for it.'

'Be quiet, Botley,' Mr Grimwade snapped.

'I'll write a new rap for the contest,' Rocky proclaimed, 'and it'll be a lot better than that *Who's in the House?* rubbish.'

'Can we be contestants, Amber?' Chelsea asked eagerly.

'Ooh, me too,' Sharelle muscled in. 'I'd pay to be in that!'

'And me.'

'Me too.'

See? I knew it! All our friends wanted to be involved. This was going to be a *real* money-spinner for an absolutely brilliant cause. So why couldn't Dad, Auntie, Uncle Jai and Mr Grimwade see it?

'I think that perhaps it's time you all went home now,' Auntie said calmly. 'Thank you for coming.'

'But what about our takeaway from the Tip-Top Tandoori?' Jazz asked in a disappointed voice.

'*Honestly*, Jazz,' Geena said. 'Amber has just opened her big mouth and dropped herself right in it for about the next twenty years, and all you can think of is food.'

'But I'm hungry,' Jazz complained.

The atmosphere had oh-so-definitely gone a bit flat now. Mr Grimwade muttered something to Uncle Jai and then stomped out. George winked at me and followed, but not before whispering in my ear, 'I'll be a contestant, if you like.'

I didn't answer. The thought of being locked up with George Botley for any length of time, while scary, wasn't my major problem at the moment. My first task was to make sure that this event went ahead *at all*.

'Just make sure your competition is very taste-ful, Amber,' Mrs Dhaliwal warned me as she left with Mr Attwal. 'None of this bad language and half-naked girls.'

'You could ask some local businesses to sponsor you,' Mr Attwal suggested. 'I'll provide the food for the contestants if I can have a banner outside the school: ATTWAL'S MARVELLOUS MINIMARKET! THE FRESHEST, THE BEST, THE CHEAPEST—'

'Goodnight,' Uncle Jai said firmly, ushering them out.

Finally just Dad, Auntie, Uncle Jai, Geena, Jazz and Baby were left. And me. Baby was lolling in her chair with a look of enjoyment on her face, obviously anticipating a tremendous scene.

'Sorry for just coming out with it like that,' I said. (I wasn't, but I figured lying was surely the best policy here.) 'I should have asked first.'

'I don't think this is a good time to talk at the moment,' Dad replied quietly. 'We're all tired and emotional. We'll discuss this tomorrow.'

Geena and Jazz looked at me sympathetically.

'You are so dead, Amber,' Baby said with glee, and strolled out.

Maybe I was. But if I could convince Dad, Auntie and Uncle Jai that my mad, my crazy, my downright lunatic idea might just work, then maybe Mr Morgan (gulp) would take me seriously too.

It was my only chance.

'Time to have that talk, Amber,' said Dad in a deadly serious voice.

He, Auntie and Uncle Jai had just marched into the living room, looking as doom-laden as the Four Horsemen of the Apocalypse. OK, so there were only three of them, but you know what I mean.

I tried not to panic. I hadn't got a lot of sleep last night because I'd been planning and re-planning what I was going to say. And how I was going to convince them that this ridiculous idea would work.

I was still panicking even now as Dad, Auntie and Uncle Jai sat down in a grim-faced row on the sofa. Dad didn't usually need reinforcements when it came to telling us off, but I guessed that Uncle Jai was present because it involved the school. Auntie was there because she could never keep her nose out of anything.

'You two had better leave,' Dad told Geena and Jazz, who were sprawled on the sofa in their jim-jams. Thankfully, Baby was still snoring away upstairs.

'Can we just see the local news?' asked Jazz. 'It's on in two minutes.'

The atmosphere in the room, already chilly, became decidedly frosty. We sat in tense silence, watching a string of stupid ads, waiting for the news. Two minutes felt like two hours. I wondered how I'd feel if they decided not to show my interview after all. It would probably *slightly* reduce the amount of trouble I was in, but on the other hand, I wanted the publicity. It might help me to convince Mr Morgan to go for it.

Finally the local news began, with newsreader Preeti Desai. Without speaking, we watched boring reports about a robbery in the Broadway shopping centre, people protesting about the site of a new housing estate and the visit of an MP.

Then we came to the *really* interesting news.

'Local residents were celebrating last night as Bollywood star Molly Mahal won the reality TV show *Who's in the House?*,' Preeti declared. 'Martha Rigby reports.'

'Molly Mahal was once a major Bollywood star,' Martha began. She was standing against a very familiar background which I eventually realized was our front garden. 'Earlier this year, when she was down on her luck, she spent several months in the area, staying with her friends, the Dhillon family. Now, of course, her career is back on track, and last night's win was the icing on the cake. And the Dhillons and their friends were only too happy to celebrate Molly's victory.'

I sat forward in my seat as the clip of Kieron King reading out the result was shown. This was followed by a swift cutaway to everyone jumping up and down in our living room, cheering. Neither Geena, Jazz nor I dared to say anything. The picture moved back to show Molly exiting the house to cheers and applause. I hadn't seen any of that yesterday because I'd caused such uproar. Then there was a close-up of Jazz and Dad, and

Jazz let out a squeak of pleasure, but didn't risk saying anything else.

'And not only are they celebrating Molly's victory, but the family are also planning their very own *Who's in the House?* style contest!' Martha declared enthusiastically. 'As Ambajit Dhillon explained to us . . .'

Whoops. I just hoped Mr Grimwade wasn't choking on his porridge.

And there I was, in close-up on the screen, telling everyone about my idea.

Ten contestants, including myself and my sisters, will be locked up inside Coppergate School . . .

Now it was *real*. It was out there. Could I pull it off?

'Sounds like a great fund-raising idea, doesn't it?' Martha declared. 'We'll definitely keep you posted! This is Martha Rigby reporting from—'

Dad snapped off the TV. 'Time to go,' he said to Geena and Jazz in a tone that brooked no argument.

The two of them scrambled off the sofa, giving me sympathetic looks, and went out.

Silence.

'Ambajit,' said Dad. Note the full name. Oh dear, this was bad. 'What have you got to say for yourself?'

I squirmed a bit.

'Mr Grimwade phoned Mr Morgan immediately, and he called us last night,' Uncle Jai said.

'*After* we'd gone to bed,' Auntie added. 'Mr Morgan wants to see you first thing on Monday morning.'

'Look, I'm sorry,' I said. 'I didn't think things through. But now that I *have*, I know it could work. I really do.'

Three pairs of eyebrows shot up.

'I know my idea sounds ridiculous, but we can't possibly raise all the money we need by Christmas,' I went on, 'unless we go for something really big. You saw how our mates were yesterday – they all want to be in the contest! I think it could be a great laugh, and I know we could raise lots of money this way. Otherwise we'd have to ask Dad to pay, and we really want to do this ourselves. For Mum . . .'

I stopped, horrified to hear my voice wobbling a bit. I hadn't meant to play the sympathy vote, but all three of them were now looking marginally less stern.

'All right, Ambajit,' Dad said coolly. 'Let's *assume*, just for one crazy moment, that this could actually happen. How do you think it would work?'

I brightened a little. I knew that they just wanted to point out to me exactly why it *couldn't* work, but I was confident I could answer most of their objections. I'd gloss over the rest.

'Well, I though we could do it at the end of term. There'd be ten pupils who are contestants—'

'Forget it, Amber,' Auntie interrupted. 'Ten pupils locked up without any adult supervision? No chance.'

'OK.' That was my ideal scenario, but I'd never really thought it would be allowed. So then I played my ace. 'Well, there's six of *us*, for a start.'

'Us?' Dad repeated.

'Yep.' I ticked the family off on my fingers. 'You, me, Auntie, Uncle Jai, Geena and Jazz.'

They stared at me as the penny dropped.

'You want *us* to take part?' Auntie said, looking utterly astounded.

'Well, yes,' I replied, wide-eyed.

That had floored them, just as I'd hoped. If all those adults were there to look after us, what could *possibly* go wrong?

Auntie was first to rally.

'We wouldn't really be contestants though,' she said. 'We'd just be there to supervise. No one's going to be interested in us adults.'

'You have to be joking,' I replied. 'You and

Uncle Jai are Coppergate celebrities, especially since you got married. Everyone loves you to bits. It's Dad no one's going to be interested in. But I thought it would be nice to have him along.'

'How kind,' said Dad, raising his eyebrows.

'Baby would have to come too,' Auntie pointed out. 'Her parents don't come back till Christmas Eve.'

'What?' That had never even occurred to me. 'Her school won't let her have time off, will they?'

'It's a private school so they finish earlier than you,' Auntie reminded me. 'She'll already be on holiday.'

'Oh, right,' I said slowly. It had only taken a moment or two for me to realize that maybe it wasn't such a *bad* thing. Baby, with her tantrums, pouts, sulks and skimpy outfits, might prove as much of a draw as Romy Turner had. 'Well – OK, then. That's seven of us.'

'Amber, there are a lot of health and safety issues to consider,' Uncle Jai said. 'There's the whole question of people staying overnight in the school, for one thing—'

'Oh, didn't the sixth-formers hold a sponsored sleepover in their block a few months ago?' I interrupted smoothly. 'That's *exactly* why I was thinking that we could hold the competition in the sixth-form building. It's separate from the rest of the school and it's got its own kitchen and all that.'

'And where would the sixth-formers go?' asked Auntie as Uncle Jai blinked several times, probably astounded by my brilliant forward planning.

'Well, if we held the contest near the end of term, most of the sixth-formers don't even bother coming in then,' I replied.

'That's true,' Uncle Jai agreed, then looked embarrassed.

'And we wouldn't do it for weeks on end, like the TV programme,' I went on.

'Thank God for that,' Auntie remarked.

'Just for maybe five days, Monday to Friday.'

'You seem to have this all thought out, Amber,' said Dad. He said *Amber*. Good sign!

'I have, Dad.' I stared hopefully at him. 'The school's got TV cameras and webcams and loads of TVs and computers. I'm not exactly sure yet how the filming would work, but I bet Mrs Cartwright and Mr Okenuwe could sort it all out.'

'The heads of media studies and IT,' Uncle Jai supplied helpfully.

'We'd be filmed, and then they could edit the film for everyone in the school to watch the same day,' I explained further. 'Maybe they could show it after school or something. And the contestants could do challenges, like the TV programme.'

'And how, exactly, is this going to raise any money?' asked Dad.

'Well, people would pay to vote for their favourite contestants,' I replied confidently. I'd seen just how enthusiastic all our friends were yesterday. 'They could pay a pound to vote after every challenge, just like the TV programme. There are about fifteen hundred pupils at Coppergate, so if they all vote just once, that's fifteen hundred pounds!' I looked round at them, hoping that they were impressed. 'And even if only half of them ever vote, maybe they'll vote two, or three, or more times, which will be . . .' I screwed up my face as I tried to do a load of calculations in my head, but I quickly gave up. 'Well, a lot of money, anyway.'

Dad, Auntie and Uncle Jai were trying not to look too interested, but I could see that they were intrigued, to say the least. Hurrah!

'No evictions though,' Auntie said sternly. 'That could end up with all the grown-ups being voted out first.'

'Fine,' I agreed breezily. 'No evictions. We just announce the winner, the person who gets the most votes throughout the week, on the Friday.'

They all fell silent. Did I have a glimmer of hope?

'This is still the most ridiculous thing I've ever heard,' Dad said, shaking his head. 'What did I ever do to deserve such a crazy daughter?' But he was smiling ever so slightly.

'Well, what do you think?' I dared to say.

'I think . . .' Dad paused and I waited hopefully. 'I think that, against all the odds, it *might* just work—'

'Thanks, Dad!' I screamed, leaping to my feet.

Dad held up a hand. 'But, Amber, it's not us you have to convince. It's Mr Morgan . . .'

'When's the *Who's in the House?* contest, Amber?'

'Can I be in it?'

'Me too!'

'And me!'

The clamour and the crush at the school gates were unbelievable on Monday morning. Geena, Jazz and I, along with Kiran and Kim, couldn't even get *through* them, there were so many kids hanging around waiting for me.

'See?' I yelled at the others. 'I knew this was a great idea!'

'I still think you're mad,' Kim replied, almost

lifted off her feet by the pressure of the crowd.

'So did I,' Geena shouted, 'but I'm coming round to it.'

'Well, I think it's fab,' Jazz shrieked. 'All these idiots want to give us their money.'

'Not quite so loud, please, Jazz,' I muttered.

Kiran began shouldering her way through the mob and we followed in her wake like celebrities behind a bodyguard. If I'd had any doubts before today, they'd vanished completely this morning. It looked like almost everyone in the whole school wanted to be involved. Even Baby, when she'd found out she'd have to come too, hadn't been *that* snooty about it.

'I knew I was right!' I said triumphantly. 'This is going to be the greatest event ever in the glorious history of Coppergate School!'

'Or possibly the greatest number of detentions ever handed out to a single person at Coppergate School,' Geena remarked.

I didn't understand what she meant until I saw Mrs Capstick standing outside the school office. She was not smiling. Grimly she beckoned me to follow her.

'Oh dear.' I felt a little of my confidence and bravery seep away. 'I suppose I'd better go and see Morgan and get it over with.'

'Can I have your locker if you're expelled?' asked Jazz.

Mrs Capstick did not say a word as she marched me along to Mr Morgan's office. I strode in rather more confidently than I felt and Mrs Capstick closed the door behind me with an indignant bang.

'Ambajit,' Mr Morgan said coldly, staring at me over his glasses, 'I'm waiting for a satisfactory explanation for your extraordinary behaviour on Friday night.'

'Well, you *did* say you liked to see Coppergate pupils showing initiative, sir,' I replied.

'Not *that* much initiative,' Mr Morgan snapped. 'Of all the silly, ridiculous, downright irresponsible things to do . . .'

'You're alive!' Jazz said when I tottered out of Mr Morgan's office a gruelling twenty minutes later. She sounded slightly disappointed. 'What happened?'

'He gave me a right telling-off for about five minutes,' I replied, squirming as I remembered some of the choice phrases Mr Morgan had used. 'He practically roasted me alive.'

'Well?' said Geena. 'Are you suspended? Expelled? Permanently in detention until you leave school?'

'None of the above.' I managed a grin. 'Guess what? Morgan eventually admitted that he rang the TV company to get the interview pulled, and they somehow persuaded him not to. They've asked him to allow the competition to go ahead, and they want to come and film the preparations and then do a special news report about it.'

'Oh, let me guess,' said Geena, rolling her eyes. 'After ripping you to shreds, Mr Morgan secretly wanted the contest to happen all along?'

'Of course he does,' Jazz butted in. 'He *lurves* that kind of publicity for the school.'

'But he still had to tell Amber off because she did a very stupid thing,' Kim added.

'Thank you for your input, Kim,' I replied with a glare. 'Mr Morgan hasn't actually said yes to the contest yet, but he hasn't said no either. He told me he's thinking about it.'

The rest of my conversation with Mr Morgan had been a bit easier than the first hairy five minutes. He obviously very much liked the idea of Coppergate featuring in a special news report. On the other hand, I could tell that he was pretty nervous in case my (totally radical) fund-raising idea turned out to be a complete catastrophe. Which, if it was plastered all over the local news, could be an absolute public relations disaster for Coppergate School.

'You jammy so-and-so, Amber,' Kiran said admiringly. 'So what happened then?'

'Well, Morgan asked me how things would work and I told him my ideas,' I replied. 'He said pretty much the same stuff as Dad, Auntie and Uncle Jai. The contest can't be pupils only, and we wouldn't be allowed to vote anyone out, in case all the grown-ups get kicked out first.'

Geena nodded wisely. 'They're obviously trying to avoid some kind of nightmarish *Lord of the Flies* scenario.'

'*Lord of the* what?' asked Jazz.

'It's a famous book, Jazz, you numbskull,' Geena explained. 'A group of boys are stranded on an island after a plane crash, and they turn into savages. A couple of them are actually murdered by the others.'

'I can understand that,' Jazz replied. 'After all, we're going to be cooped up with Baby for five days.'

'So do you really think Mr Morgan's going to go for it?' asked Kim.

'I'm *almost* certain he will,' I said, ignoring the disapproval in her voice (Kim can be *so* annoyingly prim and proper at times). 'He's just trying to save face at the moment because I went public before I'd checked it out with him first. *And* I think he wants to make sure that it's been properly planned out before he gives the official go-ahead. Anyway, I think we ought to sort out our list of ten contestants, so we're ready. We have seven so far. How are we going to choose the others?'

There was silence for a moment.

'What about Rocky?' said Jazz.

'*Rocky!*' I roared. 'No flipping way!'

'Imagine being locked up with him and having to listen to his vile rapping for days on end.' Geena shuddered. 'No, thank you.'

'Look, we're supposed to be making lots of money, aren't we?' Jazz pointed out. 'We want contestants who are going to behave badly and get everyone hooked. Baby and Rocky are perfect. They argue all the time, for a start. It'll be hilarious.'

'True,' I said thoughtfully. 'And Auntie will be watching them like a hawk. It could be funny if they try a sneaky snog. OK, Rocky's in.'

'Oh, really, Amber!' Kim said in a *very* disapproving tone. 'I can see you're *not* going for the highbrow option.'

She was totally starting to get on my nerves.

'I don't know what *you're* getting so uppity about, Kimberley Henderson,' I snapped, 'because *you're* going to be one of the contestants too.'

Oops, I hadn't actually decided that yet. It had just slipped out. But Kim's prim and proper manner and constant predictions of doom and gloom could be funny for the viewers. Besides, I was secretly thinking that it might be useful for me to have someone I could rely on (meaning, someone I could boss around and force to do my bidding).

'What!' Kim gasped. 'But I don't want to.'

'Not even for our mum?' I asked pointedly.

Kim subsided into silence, looking worried.

'That's not fair,' Jazz moaned. 'If Kim's coming, then Geena and I should be allowed to have a mate each too.'

'Absolutely,' Geena agreed.

'Well, you can't because we only have one place left now,' I said, glancing at Kiran.

'No, thanks,' Kiran said quickly. 'My mum needs me at home to babysit the kids. Why don't you have a lottery or a raffle or something for the last place? It looks like almost everyone in the school wants to be a part of it, so you could raise a bit more money by charging them for buying a ticket.'

'Superb idea!' said Geena, and Jazz and I nodded.

'Now all we have to do is wait for Mr Morgan's official permission to go ahead,' I said with confidence.

'And if he decides against it, you'll have made an enormous fool of yourself on local TV for nothing,' Jazz added helpfully.

I waited impatiently all day for Mr Morgan to call me to his office and tell me his decision, but the silence from that direction was deafening. No matter. I was going to carry on laying my plans so that we were ready to go when he said yes. *If* he said yes.

Remembering what Mr Attwal had said about getting local businesses involved, I dragged Geena and Jazz down to the Broadway after school to ask around. Mr Attwal was as good as his word and promised to supply food for the contestants free, in return for advertising his minimarket. He also gave us a cheque for one hundred pounds, which was a huge surprise.

'A lovely woman, your mother,' he said warmly. 'You three are a credit to her.'

Next, we popped into some of the other shops where Mum had been a regular customer.

Everyone we spoke to either gave us donations, or promised to, and soon we were well on the way to raising another thousand pounds. With Dad's donation and the money we'd raised ourselves, we had just under three thousand pounds so far.

'I hope we don't have to give all this money back if Morgan says no,' Geena remarked, looking worried.

'Oh my goodness,' said Jazz, screeching to a halt outside the Kwality Kar Emporium. 'Look at this.'

The Kwality Kar Emporium was where Molly Mahal had taken part in the Touch the Car competition when she'd been staying with us, and the owner, Mr Gill, was a mad Molly fan. He'd pasted up film posters of Molly in the windows of the shop, as well as the front pages of the Sunday newspapers, all of which showed pictures of her celebrating her *Who's in the House?* triumph.

'Mr Gill might help,' I said hopefully, pushing open the glass doors.

Mr Gill was in a state of great excitement. Short and tubby, he bounced across the showroom towards us like an outsized rubber ball, clutching a copy of the local newspaper.

'Look, girls!' he declared. 'Our beloved Molly Mahal is everywhere, all over the newspapers, TV, radio! And now *you're* going to hold your very own *Who's in the House?* contest. Or should I say, *Who's in the School?*! I saw your interview, Amber. Very good!'

'That's right,' I said, going into my prepared speech. 'And we were wondering if you'd like to be involved . . .'

Mr Gill listened with close attention as I explained how the contest would work, and how other local businesses were sponsoring us. I did not say that Mr Morgan hadn't actually given the go-ahead yet.

'And how is the contest going to be policed?' Mr Gill asked.

'Sorry?' I said, confused.

'Well, on TV it's hilarious to see some of the contestants trying to escape from the house!' Mr Gill chuckled. 'I was wondering if you were all going to be locked up securely, like in the real pro-gramme.'

'Oh, we will be,' I replied. 'We won't be able to leave.'

'And there'll be security guards to make sure of that?' Mr Gill asked.

'Absolutely.' I didn't have a clue why he was being so insistent about security, but there didn't seem any harm in going along with it. I suppose you could call the school caretaker and his assistant 'security guards', at a push.

'Excellent!' Mr Gill beamed. 'Then, just for a bit of fun, how about if I offer a reward if one of the contestants can escape from the school, once the contest begins? Shall we say a thousand pounds?'

'Yes, let's!' I agreed, grinning from ear to ear. Jazz and Geena were wide-eyed with glee and giving me the thumbs-up.

One thousand pounds for strolling out of school halfway through the contest? I'd have some of that! This was going to be *so* easy . . .

'After much discussion with the school governors, I've come to a decision.' Mr Morgan leaned forward and eyed Jazz, Geena and me solemnly. We'd been summoned from our various classes by Mrs Capstick just before lunch the following day in order to hear the verdict. 'Due to a good deal of interest from local – and, I may say, some *national* – media, as well as local businesses, I will allow this fund-raising event to go ahead, the week before the end of term.'

'Yes!' I blurted out triumphantly, although Geena and Jazz somehow managed to contain themselves. 'Sorry, sir.'

'However,' Mr Morgan went on sternly, 'the details are still being worked out by myself and the senior teachers, and in future, everything will be co-ordinated by Mr Arora and Mr Grimwade. You will do and say *nothing* without consulting them first. Is that clear?'

We nodded, grinning sideways at each other like loons.

'And you will make up the school work you miss for those five days,' Mr Morgan added, 'during the Christmas holidays.'

Jazz turned and pulled a face at me.

'Mr Arora informs me that you wish to have a lottery for the remaining contestant in order to raise more funds.' I thought I saw a flicker of admiration for our business acumen flit across Mr Morgan's face, but I could have been mistaken. 'He and Mr Grimwade will organize that, and also make sure that anyone who wants to take part has parental consent.'

'Thank you, sir,' I said ecstatically as the lunch bell rang.

'Good luck, girls.' Mr Morgan stood up, signalling that our meeting was at an end. 'And just remember that we must maintain the good name and reputation of Coppergate School at all times.'

'Was that a veiled threat at the end there?' Geena mused as we went out.

'Probably,' I said. 'What on earth is *that*?'

A low rumbling noise was sweeping towards us down the corridor. It seemed to be coming from outside. I flung open the doors and saw a large crowd of pupils gathered there. When they saw *us*, they all started yelling questions. I staggered back slightly under the wall of noise.

'What's happening?'

'What did Mr Morgan say?'

'Is the contest going ahead?'

'Silence!' I shouted, holding up one hand.

Miraculously, the noise died away almost immediately.

'The contest *will* be going ahead near the end of term,' I announced imperiously, feeling like a Roman emperor at the gladiatorial games. The reaction was one of frenzied excitement. I waited for silence again before continuing.

'The contestants will be filmed every day and you'll be able to watch the results after school,' I explained. 'We'll be holding challenges, and you can pay to vote for your favourite contestants. The winner will be the person who has the most votes by the end of the week.'

'I think that is very likely to be me,' Jazz

murmured as the crowd broke into excited chatter again.

'Why so?' asked Geena.

Jazz looked amazed. 'It's a popularity contest,' she said, by way of explanation.

Geena glared at her. 'And your point is?'

'I'm incredibly popular,' Jazz replied with dignity.

Geena burst into mocking laughter. 'In your dreams, Jasvinder.'

'Girls, girls, girls.' I shook my finger at them. 'This might *look* like a popularity contest, but that's not the main reason for taking part, is it? Let's not forget why we're *really* doing this. To raise money for Mum.'

Geena and Jazz looked a bit embarrassed and said no more. I smiled slightly. Of course, I fully intended to win the contest myself.

'We have a place left for just one contestant,' I proclaimed. There were a few dark mutterings at this. It *had* almost been two places because Auntie and Dad had at first flatly refused to have Rocky *and* Baby. Baby, of course, had been thrilled and had told Rocky immediately. I'd finally managed to get round Dad and Auntie by pointing out that Rocky and Baby would have absolutely *no* opportunity for lovey-dovey-type behaviour as they would be with the rest of us at all times. I did not say that I was hoping for diva-style tantrums and tears, but I was sure they'd guessed that anyway.

'So we'll be holding a lottery to find that lucky person!' I went on. 'A pound per go.'

'Can we have more than one go each?' shouted George Botley, who'd somehow managed to jostle his way to the front of the crowd as usual.

'You can have as many as you like,' Jazz butted in, 'as long as you pay up.'

I gazed around with satisfaction as everyone began talking excitedly. Our event was now creating as much of a thrill as *Who's in the House?* had done. That was exactly what I'd set out to do. I just knew this was going to be the best, the biggest, the most rewarding Coppergate School fund-raiser of all time.

Not only that, I had a secret idea to raise even more money. I wasn't going to tell *anyone* my plan, not even Geena and Jazz. It was too amazing and astounding and brilliant to talk about just yet.

Besides, I wasn't at all sure that I could actually pull it off . . .

The next two weeks before the lottery draw took place were a mad, mad whirl of activity. Uncle Jai was looking after the arrangements for the lottery, and there was a constant stream of kids heading to his classroom every break time to enter. Rumours were flying around that George Botley had entered over thirty times. Meanwhile Uncle Jai was going quietly crazy, trying to ensure that everyone had got their parents to sign the consent form, as well as spotting the forgeries.

Preparations were also going ahead for the actual contest, and Mr Grimwade was working with the other senior teachers to set everything up. The sixth-formers, with much muttering and complaining, had been kicked out of their block and had moved into the main school building. Ten camp beds and blow-up lilos had been put in two of the empty classrooms (one for the boys and one for the girls). Meanwhile, Mr Attwal and Mrs Openshaw, the cook, had got together and organized the food supplies.

Not only were there the living quarters to think about, but also how we were going to be filmed, and then how the film was going to be edited quickly enough to be shown to the rest of the school at the end of the day. The IT and media studies departments were sorting that out between them. Almost every teacher and pupil in the school had become involved in some way, and

Christmas was really taking a back seat at Coppergate this year. All the talk was about the contest.

The lottery draw took place in assembly, and as Mr Morgan mounted the stage, there was a murmur of excited tension in the air. In the middle of the stage sat the huge wooden tombola that was brought out for every school fête and fair. It was stuffed with entries for the contest.

'If I pull out now, we could get Mr Morgan to draw two winners,' Kim, who was sitting next to me, whispered in my ear.

'No chance, Kimberley,' I retorted.

'As you all know, the fund-raising contest will be taking place just before the end of term,' Mr Morgan said, raising his voice above the rustle of anticipation. 'I will now draw the name of the tenth contestant.'

He gave the tombola a push, and as it spun round, I wondered just *how* many times George Botley's name was in there. For the first time I began to feel quite nervous about the unknown person who was going to be locked up with us for five whole days. Now I came to think of it, there were quite a few oddballs in school. Kevin Dwyer in Year Ten, for example, who was a Marilyn Manson fan and had been sent home for wearing black lipstick. And Renata Collins, who bred mice to feed her pet snake. Gulp.

There was a tense hush around the hall as Mr Morgan pulled out a name. He unfolded the paper and his eyebrows almost shot off the top of his head. My heart plunged. Obviously the name was that of a *total* freak.

'And the winner is . . .' Mr Morgan drew out the moment almost as dramatically as Kieron King on the TV. 'Mr Hernandez.'

'Mr Hernandez!' I shrieked, but luckily everyone else in the hall had started talking too so my protest was drowned out.

We hadn't actually excluded the teachers from entering the lottery, but we'd never dreamed that any of them would do so. On the other hand, Mr Hernandez was incredibly popular because he was mental. In a good way, obviously. Well, he would certainly liven the contest up a bit.

'Hurrah for me!' called Mr Hernandez, looking remarkably pleased with himself. 'I haven't handed in my parental consent form yet, though. Must get that sorted out!'

There was laughter and a few whoops at that. Mr Morgan raised his hand for silence, looking as if he was having ten teeth pulled without anaesthetic. I guessed he was already stressing over how he was going to cover Mr Hernandez's classes while he was locked up with the rest of us, as well as Uncle Jai's.

'Mr Grimwade would now like to have a quick word with you all,' Mr Morgan said glumly.

Mr Grimwade stood up. 'I just want to reassure those of you who are going to be parting with your hard-earned cash that this contest is going to be *properly* policed,' he announced pompously. 'The rules are very clear. The ten contestants will not be allowed *any* contact with the outside world and will not be allowed to leave the school at all for five days and four nights, except in an emergency. For example, a serious fire.'

'Oh, so a *small* fire is OK,' I whispered to Kim. 'What's Grimwade going on about anyway? This is supposed to be a bit of *fun*.'

'While we all hope that Ambajit, Geena and Jasvinder achieve their aim and raise a lot of money, we have to ensure that the rules are followed to the letter,' Mr Grimwade went on. 'We have to stop our contestants breaking out, but we also have to stop outsiders breaking *in*.' He smiled smugly. 'For that reason, I have enlisted the services of the caretaker and his assistant, and some of the teachers, as well as a large group of sixth-formers, led by Gareth Parker and Soo-Lin

Pang. They will be in charge of security, day and night.'

'He's got to be kidding!' I muttered. Jazz, who was a few rows in front of me, had turned round and was staring at me in dismay. I turned to look at Geena, whose mouth was a round O of horror, and caught Gareth Parker's eye. He looked grim and forbidding, and like he'd never heard the words *a bit of fun.*

This was rather disastrous. This would be Gareth Parker's supreme revenge. He and his minions would make sure we were well and truly holed up without *any* possibility of escape.

So how was I going to make sure that I won Mr Gill's thousand pounds reward?

But desperate times call for very desperate measures. As we filed out of the hall, I slipped out of line, hung back for a second or two and waited for George Botley to stroll past. Then I grabbed his arm and hauled him out of sight round the corner.

'Hey, Amber.' George grinned broadly. 'If you wanted a kiss, you only had to ask.'

'Be quiet, George, and listen carefully,' I snapped.

'Ooh, I like masterful women,' George said with a wink.

I tried not to glare at him. Much as I hated to

admit it, George Botley was my one and only faint hope.

'George, I have another task for you,' I announced urgently. 'When the contest begins, you have to get me out of the school, even if it's just for five minutes. I don't care how you do it. *But you have to get me out.*'

Chapter Nine

'How much *longer* do we have to wait?' Baby complained, pulling out her make-up mirror and studying her reflection for the hundredth time. 'I'm bored.'

She twisted round and poked Rocky, who was listening to his iPod, hard in the ribs.

'Ouch!' he groaned, doubling up in pain. 'What did you do that for?'

Baby grabbed both headphone wires and yanked them out of his ears. 'I'm bored! Talk to me!' she demanded.

Rocky glared at her and made an elaborate show of zipping his mouth shut, like the teacher used to make us do in reception class.

'Oh, you're so childish!' Baby snarled.

'I want to kill the pair of them already and the contest hasn't even started yet,' Geena said in my ear.

It was the Great Day. All ten contestants were gathered in one of the classrooms in the main part of the school, awaiting our triumphal procession across to the sixth-form block. I could hardly believe that it was really happening – *today* – after all the days of planning and preparation.

'I'm scared of being locked up,' Kim moaned. 'You know how I get claustrophobic.'

'Maybe you'll have a panic attack,' Jazz suggested helpfully. 'You might win sympathy votes.'

Dad was pacing nervously up and down. Uncle Jai was trying to sit still and keep calm, but he kept jumping up to stare out into the playground. A large crowd had gathered, mostly pupils and teachers, but also some local residents, including Mr Attwal, Mrs Dhaliwal and Mr Gill. We'd been promised even more money from local businesses, and their publicity banners were draped along the playground railings. A local news crew had turned up with a camera and were interviewing Mr Morgan. I recognized Martha Rigby and the two men who'd come to our house.

'Well, here we all are, Amber,' Auntie remarked. 'Let's hope this whole thing is a huge success. And not just a huge mistake.'

I knew what she meant. How had I managed to

pull this off? It was as much of a mystery to me as to everyone else.

And then there was my extra-special, secret plan. True, I still wasn't sure if it would actually happen yet, because it all depended on someone else. But if it did, it would be absolutely *amazing*.

I was so excited, I felt sick.

'Jai, will you *please* sit down,' Auntie snapped as he went over to peer out of the window yet again. 'You're just making us all feel more nervous.'

Uncle Jai glared at her. 'I fail to see how me walking over to the window is affecting anyone else,' he said, quite huffily. Which was not at *all* like him.

The preparations for the contest had been so frantic that I'd completely forgotten my suspicions that something wasn't quite right with Auntie and Uncle Jai. But now that I thought about it, he'd been staying late at school almost every evening over the last few weeks. Of course, there had been a lot of arrangements to make for the contest. But still, they *had* only just got married. It was a bit worrying.

I glanced over at Geena and Jazz, who both raised their eyebrows at me. Kim was squirming in her seat, looking very embarrassed. Of course, we were all too polite to say anything.

'Ooh, what's going on with you two, then?' Baby exclaimed nosily.

Auntie and Uncle Jai ignored her. Pity, as the rest of us were also dying to find out what was going on. Because something obviously *was*.

'This is going to be very strange,' Dad remarked, taking out his mobile and checking it for messages. 'No TV, no radio, no phones, no emails for five whole days.'

'I bet your girlfriend's going to miss you, Uncle,' Baby said sweetly.

'Baby!' Jazz snarled.

'It was a *joke*,' Baby said in an injured tone. Dad shook his head sternly at her and put his phone away.

'I wonder who's going to come second in the contest,' Baby went on idly, taking out her make-up mirror again.

'That's an odd thing to say.' Geena frowned. 'Don't you mean, you wonder who's going to win?'

'Well, *hello*.' Baby stared at her in genuine amazement. 'I'm going to win, of course.'

'Says who?' Rocky interjected.

'It's obvious, isn't it?' Baby shrugged. 'The best-looking person's bound to win.'

'That would be me then,' Rocky said confidently.

'Like Amber said, this isn't a popularity contest,' Jazz pointed out. 'It's all about raising money for the library.'

'It *so* doesn't matter who wins,' Geena added.

'Oh, get out of here!' Baby scoffed. 'Like Amber doesn't want to win the whole thing herself!'

I wriggled uncomfortably as everyone turned to stare at me. 'Jazz is right,' I said loftily. 'It's the taking part, not the winning, that matters.'

'You sound like Molly Mahal,' Baby jeered.

'I think Baby's the one who's got it right,' Kim, the traitor, put in. 'Don't tell me you three aren't *all* desperate to win.'

I turned on her. 'Kim, you are supposedly my best friend and I'm relying on you to back me up during the contest,' I snapped.

Kim looked mutinous. 'Maybe I want to win it myself.'

'Oh, let's stop messing around!' Jazz howled. 'We *all* want to win it. There, I've said it!'

We slumped into silence again, glaring at each other. The tension was rising visibly.

The only one of us who looked completely calm was Mr Hernandez. Wearing a green shirt patterned with yellow pineapples, he was perched on a chair with his legs strangely contorted underneath him.

'Yoga,' he informed me, breathing deeply through his nose. 'It helps to keep me sane.'

'Not very effective then, is it?' Jazz said in a low voice.

Suddenly the door of the classroom flew open. We all jumped, and Mr Hernandez, unable to extricate his legs fast enough, toppled off the chair.

'Time to go,' Mr Grimwade announced. He looked quite excited himself. 'Follow me.'

We all picked up the one small suitcase we were allowed to take (oh, what a huge scene there had been when Baby found *that* out) and went after Mr Grimwade. I was hoping to be first – after all, it *had* been my idea – but Baby was closest to the door. Now she sashayed out into the playground on her highest heels, waving at the assembled crowd like the Queen. We all trailed after her like ladies-in-waiting.

'Our contestants are ready!' announced Mr Grimwade.

Applause and cheers.

'Amber, you must be very excited.' Martha Rigby thrust her microphone under my nose. 'This is a big event for your school, and for you! Tell us how you're feeling right now?'

'Nervous but excited,' I began before I was elbowed unceremoniously out of the way by Baby.

'Watch this space,' Baby purred, beaming at the camera, 'because I'm going to win!'

'Oh, she's going to be even more unbearable if she *does* win,' Geena muttered.

'Don't worry,' I said, trying to ignore the ranks of boys staring admiringly at Baby in her skinny jeans, 'she won't. The airheads never do.'

Mr Morgan was trying to quieten the crowd down so that he could make a speech or something, but everyone was just too excited and they wouldn't shut up. Looking rather fed up, he simply shouted, 'Let the competition begin! And good luck to all the contestants!' Then he stared at me rather hard. I wondered if he was wishing me *particularly* good luck, but sadly I think it was more of a warning. *If this is a disaster, you are so dead, Ambajit Dhillon . . .*

Mr Grimwade led the way over to the sixth-form block and the crowd dashed along behind us. Gareth Parker and his minions were gathered outside waiting for us, Gareth stern and un-smiling, although the others, including Soo-Lin, looked quite thrilled.

We went inside after Mr Grimwade, followed by Gareth and the sixth-formers. Gareth and Soo-Lin then banged the doors shut behind us and made a great show of locking and bolting them. The last thing I saw as the doors closed was George Botley in the crowd, winking and giving me the thumbs-up. I just hoped I hadn't made a ghastly mistake asking him to help me. But no way was I going to miss out on Mr Gill's thousand pounds . . .

'Right, you know the rules,' Mr Grimwade said briskly, ushering us into the nearest classroom. 'No mobile phones, no books, no magazines, writing materials, no personal stereos, no laptops, etc.'

Gareth immediately reached over and plucked the iPod straight out of Rocky's hand.

'Oi! Give that back, Four-Eyes!' Rocky snapped. But wilted immediately under Mr Grimwade's beady eye.

We all lined up to hand over our mobile phones. As we did so, one of them went off. The ringtone was *You're Beautiful*.

'Typical,' Jazz muttered as Baby dived into her designer handbag.

We all waited for Baby to answer her phone. But she didn't. Curiously, she took one look at the screen and let out a stifled exclamation (possibly a swear word but we couldn't quite hear). Looking completely flummoxed, she stabbed frantically at the off button. Then she tossed the phone into the box on top of the other mobiles, as if it had scalded her.

'You could have taken the call, Baby,' Mr Grimwade said mildly.

'No, that's OK,' Baby muttered, still looking flustered.

I remembered the mysterious phone call she'd had on the morning of the *Who's in the House?* finale. The one that had put her in a really bad mood. I wondered if this call was from the same person, whoever that might be. Ha! Another mystery for me to think about. And I was going to have a lot more time on my hands from now on to come up with possible solutions . . .

Rocky was looking suspicious. 'Was that a call from another guy?' he demanded. 'Are you two-timing me?'

'No, so shut up!' Baby snarled, giving him a shove.

Gareth Parker stepped quickly (and, I have to admit, quite bravely) between them. 'We'll need to search your suitcases next, of course,' he announced, obviously relishing his role as jailer.

Auntie eyeballed him sternly. 'Young man, no one is going through *my* lingerie,' she informed him.

'Nor mine,' Geena snapped.

'I don't mind you looking at *mine*, Gareth,' Baby said, batting her eyelashes and flirting outrageously.

'I meant, Soo-Lin and the girls will check *your* suitcases,' Gareth blustered.

Soo-Lin and some of the other sixth-form girls led Auntie, Kim, Baby, Geena, Jazz and me away into the adjoining classroom.

'What's all this flirting with Gareth Parker?' I asked Baby as we unlocked our suitcases. 'If you're trying to get round him somehow, it won't work. That guy's made of granite.'

'He's kind of cute though, isn't he?' Baby remarked. 'Sort of all dark and brooding. Like Heathrow.'

'I think you mean Heathcliff,' I replied. I suppose Gareth *was* actually quite attractive if you looked closely. But you had to stare *hard* to see it.

After our suitcases had passed inspection, Mr Grimwade, Gareth and Soo-Lin led us off to the sixth-form common room, which was to be our base for the next five days. We were all filing down the corridor behind them when something very dramatic happened. Quite unexpectedly, Baby stopped dead in the middle of the corridor, flung her arm out and pointed straight at Geena.

'Geena's hiding something!' she proclaimed. 'She's trying to smuggle it into the contest!'

We all swivelled to stare at Geena. She had flushed deep red in the space of just one and a half seconds.

'I am not,' she protested.

'What are you talking about, Baby?' Gareth asked sternly. 'Everybody's bags have been checked, and they're fine.'

'It's not in her bag, whatever it is,' Baby replied, flashing him a sweet smile. 'It's in her hand. *That* one. It's something white.'

We all stared down at Geena's left hand, which was tightly clenched.

'Oh, *this*,' Geena said in a would-be casual tone, opening her hand very slightly to reveal a screwed-up bit of white paper. 'It's just a good-luck note someone passed me in the playground, that's all.'

Jazz whipped round to glance at me. 'I bet it was *him*!' she whispered in my ear. 'Geena's secret boyfriend!'

'I'll take charge of that,' Gareth said sternly, whisking the note out of Geena's hand.

As we all went off down the corridor again, Jazz and I hung back so that we could have a private gossip.

'Was Geena talking to anyone when we crossed the playground just now?' I asked urgently.

'I don't know,' Jazz wailed. 'I wasn't looking.'

'How frustrating,' I muttered. Geena's mysterious love-life was something else I'd almost forgotten about during the preparations for the contest. 'Jazz, we simply *have* to find out what's going on.'

'I'm up for that,' Jazz replied enthusiastically.

The sixth-form common room was large and spacious with a kitchen at one end of it. I was intrigued to see that fixed cameras had been set up all around the room in different positions. It looked as if we could be filmed wherever we were. Black-out blinds covered the windows to make sure that no one could see in from outside, and lights had been brought over from the TV studio in the drama department. The classrooms that were doubling up as bedrooms were on either side of the common room, and there were two sets of showers and toilets too.

As we looked around, I quickly realized that, as the common room was the only place with cameras, anything we said or did outside there would not be filmed. Interesting. I could be all sweetness and light in the common room, and say and do what I liked outside it.

'As you can see, you can only be filmed when you're in here,' Gareth explained smoothly. 'However, we intend to deduct votes from anyone who spends too much time outside the common room. Apart from when you're asleep, of course.'

'How much time is too much time?' I demanded.

'We'll be the judges of that,' Gareth declared pompously.

'You're enjoying this, aren't you?' I accused. 'That's because you're a narrow-minded, annoying, swotty little—'

'Amber,' Soo-Lin interrupted, 'we *have* actually started filming.'

'What!' I gasped. Sure enough, the green camera lights were *on* – I just hadn't noticed.

'This is only a test – right?' I asked, beginning to sweat just a little.

Gareth shook his head in a superior manner. 'No, we've already done lots of test shots.' He smirked. 'We decided to switch the cameras on before you came in. To get some *candid* shots.'

I didn't zip my mouth shut as Rocky had done earlier, but I clamped my lips together firmly.

Now that I *knew* we were being filmed, I could watch what I said and did. But I already had an uncomfortable feeling that it wasn't going to be as easy in practice as it sounded in theory . . .

'We'll leave you to settle in.' Mr Grimwade headed for the door, followed by Soo-Lin and Gareth, who was still grinning triumphantly. 'But I'll be in touch soon with your very first challenge. Good luck.'

'And don't bother trying to escape,' Gareth called over his shoulder. 'There'll be a group of teachers and sixth-formers watching what's going on here in the common room at all times. All the other doors on this corridor will be locked, apart from your sleeping quarters and the shower rooms. We'll be leaving the main doors unlocked, just in case there's an emergency, but there'll be someone on guard outside, day and night. And people will be patrolling around the building too. Goodbye.'

The door banged shut behind them. We all stood there a bit awkwardly for a moment, staring at each other and at the cameras. It was actually quite hard to take in the fact that our every move was being filmed.

'Are you OK, Kim?' I asked. She was looking ever so slightly green.

'Not really.' She swallowed hard. 'It's just knowing that we can't get out if we want to.'

'Oh, I wouldn't worry about that—' I began, but stopped myself abruptly. I'd been *about* to say that I didn't believe there would be security around the building day *and* night, whatever Gareth Parker said. I didn't want to say it on camera, though.

'Oh, this is going to be such fun!' Baby announced merrily, sinking into a chair right in front of one of the cameras and directing a toothy smile straight at it. 'I'm *so* looking forward to it – and it's for *such* a good cause.'

She was almost as good an actress as Molly Mahal.

'I've written a special *Who's in the School?* rap,' Rocky boasted, moving in front of her to hog the camera. 'I reckon I ought to do it now, to start the contest off properly.'

'Oh, I think we should unpack first and get settled in,' Geena said quickly.

Suddenly there was a knock on the door. We all jumped so high we almost hit the ceiling, and Baby let out a melodramatic shriek. I dashed over and flung open the door to find Gareth Parker standing outside, holding a large cardboard box. We glared at each other.

'These are the materials for your first challenge,' Gareth snapped, thrusting the box at me. 'And we want everything back that isn't used. Oh, and we've counted all the pens and pencils, so don't bother trying to nick any.'

'But what's the challenge?' I called as Gareth stomped off down the corridor.

'*ATTENTION, CONTESTANTS!*'

The booming voice of Mr Grimwade over the loudspeaker system bounced off the walls of the room and nearly deafened us.

'*Er – I think you need to turn it down slightly, sir,*' we heard Soo-Lin say.

'*Ah, yes . . .*' There was silence for a moment or two, and then Mr Grimwade's voice was back, a bit lower but not much. '*Contestants, we have your first challenge!*'

'Ooh, sock it to us!' Mr Hernandez called. 'We're ready!'

'*The challenge is to make yourself a fancy-dress costume from anything you can find lying around the common room and the classrooms,*' Mr Grimwade went on. '*We've given you some basic materials in the box Gareth has just delivered. The sixth-formers and I will be awarding points for the best costumes and, of course, your efforts will also be voted for by the rest of the school. You have one hour – starting NOW!*'

There was a second's pause before we all stormed into action, apart from Baby, who remained in her chair, fluttering her eyelashes at the camera.

'Look!' I flung the cardboard box open and began pulling stuff out. 'Tissue paper! Staplers! Glue! Card! Paints!'

'Ooh, give me some!' Jazz declared, launching herself at me. 'I've had a fab idea!'

We shared out the stuff in the box, and then Kim and I disappeared into the girls' classroom to get started, leaving Auntie, Uncle Jai and Dad poking around the common room, looking for inspiration. Meanwhile, Rocky and Mr Hernandez had already got to work in the other classroom.

Geena and Jazz joined Kim and me after a while, and we all had such a laugh making our costumes. Even Kim cheered up a bit. We could also hear raised voices and gales of laughter coming from the common room next door. I felt pleased and also quite proud of myself. This was turning out *exactly* the way I'd planned.

When Mr Grimwade called us together again an hour later, there was more hysterical laughter. I was a daisy and Kim was a buttercup. We'd wrapped ourselves in green tissue paper and wore white and yellow cardboard petal head-dresses. Jazz had made herself a fairy costume with a rather snazzy glittery wand, and Geena was a hula-girl in a tissue-paper grass skirt and a paper-flower garland.

'Where have the sofa cushions gone?' asked Jazz, glancing round the common room. 'And all the throws?'

An Indian maharajah and his maharani (Uncle Jai and Auntie) paraded into the room and we all applauded. Uncle Jai was wearing one of the sofa throws and a very dashing turban made from a tea towel. Auntie had very painstakingly wound herself into a tissue-paper sari and had a red-paint bindi. Their servant (Dad) followed behind them, wearing the other sofa throw and wafting them with his palm fan, which was actually a broom handle with cardboard leaves stuck on one end of it.

'I can't wait to see what Baby's wearing,' Geena muttered in my ear. Baby had worked on her costume on her own in the girls' shower room. She'd been intensely secretive and had refused to let anyone see it.

'*We're still waiting for three of our contestants!*' Mr Grimwade yelled over the loudspeaker.

We all winced.

'I wish he'd stop doing that,' Jazz complained.

'*We shall be deducting votes if you don't show your-selves NOW!*' Mr Grimwade added menacingly.

Rocky rushed in from the guys' classroom. His outfit must have taken him, oh – all of five minutes to get ready. He wore a T-shirt, shorts and trainers, all of which I guessed he'd brought with him, and he'd wound strips of white tissue paper around his hands.

'I'm a boxer,' he explained as we all looked blank. 'You know, like in the *Rocky* movies?'

He bounced across the room with some fancy footwork and aimed a pretend jab in Auntie's direction. She glared at him.

'Oh, are you all waiting for little old me?' Baby called, slinking into the room. She was wearing a cut-off T-shirt, a tissue-paper veil across the lower half of her face and a tissue-paper skirt with a long slit up one side. We all goggled at her. Her skirt was rather revealing.

'I'm a belly dancer,' Baby explained patiently, shimmying across the room.

'Baby, go and put your jeans on, *now*,' Auntie snapped, moving swiftly to cut her off as she headed for the nearest camera. 'That skirt is almost see-through.'

'Oh, really?' Baby said with pretend innocence. 'I didn't realize.'

Auntie bundled her quickly out of the room, and at the same moment we heard Mr Hernandez yelling for help. We ran out and found him wedged in the doorway of the guys' classroom. Not surprising, seeing that he'd strapped the purple sofa cushions to himself, front, back and sides, and was about five times the size he'd been before. He also had a strange cardboard triangle attached to his head and was carrying Auntie's handbag.

'What *are* you meant to be, sir?' asked Geena as we helped to push him through the door.

'I'm a Teletubby,' Mr Hernandez panted.

Of course. It was obvious once you knew. We could hardly stand up for laughing as we shoved him through the door and into the common room. Mr Grimwade could barely say anything over the loudspeaker, he was chuckling so hard, and we could hear the sixth-formers laughing hysterically in the background. It looked like Mr Hernandez had probably won the most votes from them, then – although there would still be voting by the rest of the school taking place later this afternoon, when they watched the first day's filming.

'*The first challenge is now over,*' Mr Grimwade announced. '*We'll be in touch with you again to-morrow. But don't worry, we'll still be keeping an eye on you all!'* Then the loudspeaker system clicked off and there was silence.

We all stood there in our ridiculous costumes and things suddenly went quite flat. I realized that there was a *long* afternoon to get through before bed time.

'How about if we have some lunch now?' asked Auntie.

'Oh, you're doing all the cooking, are you?' I said. 'Great.'

'I've drawn up a rota,' Auntie said forbiddingly. 'May I borrow my handbag, Tinky-Winky?' She took her handbag from Mr Hernandez, whisked out a piece of paper and laid it on the coffee table.

'But I can't cook,' Baby complained.

'Now is the perfect time to learn, then,' Auntie retorted, 'as we've got so much time on our hands.'

Baby flounced out of the common room in a sulk. And then shot straight back in again as she remembered that she might lose points. I grinned. She was *such* an airhead, she'd forgotten all about the cameras.

'Can you believe Baby prancing around in that see-through skirt?' Jazz muttered. 'I suppose she's going to try and grab votes by putting herself

209

about like Romy Turner did. I bet she's brought her bikini too—'

'Ssh!' Geena hissed, giving Jazz a violent poke. 'We don't want everyone getting interested in Baby!' And she nodded at the nearest camera.

'Ow, that hurt,' Jazz grumbled. She tried to slap Geena's arm but Geena parried her swiftly. So, with a neat counter-attack, Jazz trod down heavily on her toe.

'Yikes!' Geena shrieked with pain and began hopping around the common room. 'Jazz, you'll regret this.'

'Girls!' Dad said warningly.

I smiled to myself. Maybe I was going to be the *only* person who never forgot about the cameras, just like Molly Mahal on the TV. If I kept my wits about me, I could win this thing. I was sure of it. I mean, how hard could it be?

Auntie and Geena were down to make lunch, so we all sat around waiting to eat. There wasn't anything to do apart from talk to each other. Uncle Jai tried to initiate a game of I-Spy but that collapsed into chaos with Jazz's choice of 'B' for Bimbo, as a result of which Baby got the raging sulks.

After lunch it was still only 1.30 and time seemed to be crawling by. I wouldn't have believed that I could get so bored in just a few hours, but I was *desperate*. I'd have given my right arm – or, in fact, any one of my limbs – for a book, my iPod, a TV, *anything*. Kim and I went on a lightning raid around the classrooms where we were sleeping but everything had been removed. I imagined Gareth Parker chuckling with glee like a psychotic James Bond villain as he carried boxes of books away.

I have to say, I think all this boredom was already affecting my sanity.

'This is so dull,' Baby complained every five minutes, on the dot. 'I'm *so* bored.'

'I'll cheer you up,' Rocky announced at 3.10. He'd been sitting on his own in a corner since lunch, staring into space. 'I've composed a special rap for you, babe.'

'Sadly, I'm so bored, I'm actually looking forward to hearing this,' Geena murmured.

'I know,' I replied. 'Frightening, isn't it?'

Rocky cleared his throat and began to strut up and down the common room, pointing his fingers downwards in the classic rapper style.

> *'Come on honey,*
> *Give me back my money.*
> *You've borrowed so much,*
> *It just ain't funny.'*

'WHAT!' Baby screeched in a terrifying tone.

'It's taken him two hours to come up with *that*?' Jazz whispered.

Baby had leaped to her feet. Hands on hips, she bore down furiously on Rocky. 'You can take that back, you loser!' she yelled. 'I don't owe you *that* much!'

'Baby, remember the cameras—' Auntie began, but Baby was too far gone to care. This was *great*. I hadn't expected a Big Row on the first day.

'Oh now, let me see . . .' Rocky said, his voice dripping with sarcasm. 'One hundred and twelve pounds twenty-seven pence, I think.'

'Well, if you can't afford the luxury goods, stay out of the designer store!' Baby retorted, eyes flashing. 'And you can forget about meeting up tonight when everyone's asleep, you moron!'

'Oh, you can forget about that *every* night,' Dad said sternly. 'Your auntie and I both have keys to our classrooms, and the doors will be locked when we go to bed.'

'Baby, you *do* have a very generous allowance,' Auntie said. 'You ought to think about paying Rocky back.' She was right. Baby's monthly allowance from her parents was legendary – at least two hundred and fifty pounds.

'Oh, but any guy should be *glad* to pay for his

girlfriend,' I said quickly. 'Baby just wants to be treated like a lady. Right, Baby?'

'Exactly!' Baby snapped. 'You're not as stupid as you look, Amber.'

'Thank you,' I said.

Kim was staring disapprovingly at me and Auntie also gave me a penetrating stare.

'Ever heard the phrase *adding fuel to the fire*, Amber?' she asked.

'I'm sure I don't know what you mean,' I said. Well, there was no *harm* in trying to make things a bit more interesting for the viewers, was there? I did wonder why Baby kept borrowing the money in the first place, though. I mean, she was *loaded*. Or at least her parents were.

'I've made up a rap too.' Baby narrowed her eyes at Rocky.

> *'You think you're so flash*
> *But you're stingy with your cash.*
> *Don't make me cry*
> *Or I'll go find another guy!'*

Then she stomped off to the far corner of the common room.

'I think I'm going to need a long holiday to get over this week,' Geena remarked as Baby and

Rocky glowered at each other from opposite sides of the room.

'Well, Auntie and Uncle Jai are off on their honeymoon in the Christmas holidays,' I said idly. 'Maybe they'll take us with them.'

'What honeymoon?' asked Uncle Jai, looking and sounding bewildered.

There was a tense silence. For once, and this almost *never* happens, Auntie looked completely caught out.

'Our honeymoon to Australia,' she said quickly.

Uncle Jai blushed red. 'Oh, yes, I'd forgotten,' he said in a stifled voice.

'Forgotten?' I repeated in an incredulous voice. As I'd suspected before, there was definitely some mystery here. But what, WHAT, WHAT???

'I didn't know you were thinking of going to Australia,' Dad said curiously.

'We haven't worked out any of the details yet,' Auntie said, too obviously longing to drop the subject, which made me even more suspicious. 'Let's all have a nice cup of tea.'

I was thoughtful as Auntie bustled around a bit *too* much, putting the kettle on. Maybe I wasn't going to be as bored as I'd feared. My family seemed to have enough secrets to keep me busy for the next five weeks, never mind five days.

Now, at last, I had some time to find out exactly what was going on.

I woke up in the middle of the night, thinking that someone was poking me in the back with a stick. But it turned out that the camp bed I was lying on was just supremely uncomfortable.

Oh, how time had *dragged* all day. We'd actually gone to bed at 9.30 because we were so bored. Then, for the next two hours, we'd been kept awake by Baby moaning that she couldn't sleep. Now, though, there wasn't a sound in the classroom.

I tried to get back to sleep, but I started wondering what was happening outside in the real world. Had anyone turned up to watch the screening of today's filming after school was over? Everyone had been so excited this morning, surely loads of them must have come along? How many of them had voted, and how much money had we raised so far? And which one of us had got the most votes today? I just hoped the teachers and pupils who were editing the footage had cut out all the boring bits, because there were plenty of those . . .

The moon was gleaming in through the windows, throwing strange shadows around the room. I peered at my watch. It was three in the morning. Mr Grimwade and Gareth Parker wouldn't be expecting any of us to try and escape on the first night, would they? So I ought to give it a go. I wasn't going to hang around on the off-chance that George Botley might help me. However, I had a problem . . .

I crept across the room to Auntie's bed.

'Auntie?' I whispered, tapping her shoulder. 'Wake up!'

'Eh?' Auntie surfaced from a deep sleep and sat bolt upright. 'What's the matter?'

'I want to try and break out so that I can win Mr Gill's thousand quid,' I explained. 'But you've got the key to the classroom.'

Yawning, Auntie pulled the key out from under her pillow and climbed out of bed.

'You're coming too?' I said, amazed.

'You don't think I'm letting you go alone, Amber, do you?' Auntie retorted. 'Come along.'

Silently we left the classroom and Auntie re-locked the door behind her. Then we hurried down the corridor. As long as we kept out of the common room, no one would see us on camera. Anyway, I very much doubted whether any of the sixth-formers or teachers would be on duty *all* night, whatever they said. I tried every other door along the way, but they were locked, as Gareth had said.

'Do you *really* believe that Mr Grimwade's got someone on guard outside day and night?' I whispered, gazing down the corridor at the main doors. Knowing those doors were unlocked and that we could open them and walk out if we wanted to was extremely tempting.

Auntie shrugged. 'Who knows?' she replied. 'But I wouldn't be surprised.'

'Well, surely the windows must be unlocked too,' I said. 'What if there was a fire and we couldn't get to the doors?'

Auntie stopped underneath one of the windows at the end of the corridor. 'Only one way to find out,' she said.

The window ledge was a little too high for me to climb up to, so Auntie had to give me a leg-up. I lifted myself onto the ledge, panting a little, and tried the catch.

'It's not locked!' I whispered triumphantly.

I was just pushing the window open when I happened to glance down. I gave a little shriek. Gareth Parker was standing outside, looking up at me.

'Good evening, Amber,' he said sarcastically. 'Or should that be good morning?'

'Wh-what are you doing here?' I gulped.

'Don't you remember?' Gareth replied. 'We have a rota for security day *and* night. There's always a group of teachers and sixth-formers on patrol.'

'But how did you know . . . ?'

'That you'd left your sleeping quarters?' Gareth gave me a superior smile. 'There are security cameras in *all* the corridors. They were installed when the sixth-form block was built. Didn't you notice them when you moved in?'

'No,' I snapped.

'Oh dear, maybe we should have pointed them out.' Gareth shrugged. 'I suggest you go back to your room right away. You'll already lose votes for this.' Smirking slightly, he took out a walkie-talkie and spoke into it. 'Gareth to base. I've apprehended the escapees, Ms Woods. Over and out.'

Sulkily I slammed the window shut and jumped down off the ledge.

'I take it we got caught,' said Auntie.

'Yes, and now we've lost votes,' I grumbled. I hadn't realized everyone was going to take the security issue so *seriously*. I would have to rely on the cunning and intelligence of George Botley to get me out now. What a truly horrific thought. I might as well say goodbye to Mr Gill's money right here, right now.

'Well, we'd better go and get some sleep,' Auntie replied. 'We're going to need all our strength tomorrow for another day of sitting around and listening to Rocky and Baby arguing.'

'Mm, there's something funny going on there, don't you think?' I speculated. 'Why on earth is Baby borrowing so much money from him?'

We stopped outside our classroom door and Auntie turned to stare hard at me.

'Amber, just remember that whatever's going on with Baby and Rocky, or anyone else, we do *not* want to discuss family business in front of the cameras. Is that clear?'

'As crystal,' I replied quickly. I was only going to do a bit of digging around. I had to be careful myself too.

After all, I still had that BIG secret of my own that I absolutely did not want *anyone* else to know about.

Mostly because I'd look like a great big loser if it didn't come off . . .

Chapter Ten

The next day, Tuesday, started off rather badly. It took me a long time to get to sleep because I was tossing and turning for ages, planning revenge on Gareth Parker. Then, when I finally fell asleep, I had the most awful nightmare. I dreamed that it was really early in the morning and Mr Grimwade was yelling at me in his loudest voice to *GET UP*.

Groggily I opened my eyes. This was no dream.

'*Wakey, wakey, contestants!*' Mr Grimwade roared over the loudspeaker. He sounded as fresh as a daisy. '*Rise and shine! It's time for your next challenge!*'

'How can this be?' Jazz moaned, rolling off the camp bed and onto the floor with a bump. 'It's only seven o'clock.'

'This is mental and physical torture.' Geena

gave a great yawn. 'Haven't we even got time for a shower?'

'*I want to see you in the common room in five minutes!*' Mr Grimwade ordered.

Half-heartedly we began scrabbling around for our clothes. I glanced at Baby, who was apparently still asleep.

'What about her?'

'Baby!' Auntie shook her by the shoulder. 'We have to get up now.'

Baby said a rather rude word and stayed where she was, eyes firmly closed.

'Oh, leave her be,' I said. 'She won't have a hope of winning with all these points she's losing.'

Baby sat up. 'I'm coming,' she muttered, 'but there's no way I'm going in front of the cameras without my make-up.'

'*Time's running out, contestants!*' Mr Grimwade informed us gleefully.

Five minutes later we went to the common room to join Dad, Mr Hernandez, Uncle Jai and Rocky, who were slumped on the sofas, half asleep. Our next challenge turned out to be what Mr Grimwade called the Coppergate Olympics. We each had to come up with a sporting event, using stuff found around the common room and classrooms. Then we'd all have a go at the different sports everyone had invented. We'd get points for winning the events, and people could vote for their favourites too.

I was quite pleased with mine, which was a skittles game. All right, so I've never seen skittles in the real Olympics *yet*, but hey, there's a first time for everything. I made the skittles out of cardboard and the bowling balls out of scrunched-up newspaper sellotaped together. Mr Hernandez cheated a bit and held a 'How long can you stand on your head?' event. As he was into yoga, he did brilliantly at that while the rest of us failed miserably. Still, it was amusing. Or it would have been if it hadn't been quite so early in the morning.

I did pretty well in most of the other events. I came first in the 'Juggling with plastic cups' event (that was Kim's), third in Dad's Long Jump and second in the Toss the Cushion competition. That was Baby's idea and basically involved us standing at one end of the common room and seeing how many times we could hit the notice board on the opposite wall by chucking a cushion at it.

Anyway, by the end of it all, I was convinced I'd pick up plenty of votes when the next set of film footage was shown after school today, which might make up for the fact that I'd had some deducted some last night.

It was only after Mr Grimwade had signed off and Dad and I were making breakfast that I finally glanced at the clock. Setting up all the different events, then doing them, had taken quite some time. But it was still only ten past ten. Eek! *How* was I going to get through the rest of the day?

We had breakfast at 10.30. Eating breakfast took fifteen minutes. It was now 10.45. I began trying to calculate how many minutes were left before we could go to bed. Then I could count them down in my head. Oh dear, I was becoming almost as geeky as Gareth Parker.

'Dad, what do you think is happening outside?' I mused as the two of us loaded the breakfast plates into the dishwasher. 'I keep wondering if anyone's watching us. And how many people have voted.'

'And whether you're winning?' Dad asked with a teasing smile.

'No,' I began. Then grinned. 'Well, yes. What about you?'

'Get real, Amber.' Dad looked highly amused. 'No one's interested in *me*. I'll be lucky to get a single vote.'

'Thanks for coming anyway,' I said, scraping

leftover cornflakes into the bin. 'It was nice of your boss to let you have time off work.'

Dad was squinting at the dishwasher controls. 'That big engineering project was postponed a few months ago, so we're not actually that busy at the moment,' he remarked absently.

What?! Something did *not* add up here. I stared at Dad in bewilderment.

'But you've been working late for ages, Dad, right up until the contest, and you kept saying it was because of that project . . .' My voice tailed away. Dad had been telling us fibs. Why?

Dad froze, looking like he wanted to climb into the dishwasher and hide himself away. 'Oh, er – well, we're always busy, Amber. You know that.' Dad attempted a casual tone but failed horribly. And then he suddenly seemed extremely interested in rummaging through the box of dishwasher tablets.

I left him to it and rushed over to Geena and Jazz, my mind reeling with all sorts of possibilities. Many of them unpleasant.

They were sitting on one of the sofas with Kim, passing the time by plaiting Kim's long blonde hair into lots of tiny dreadlocks.

'What's the matter with you, Amber?' asked Geena. 'You look worried.'

'She knows I'm going to win the contest, that's why,' Jazz said.

'I have to talk to you – in private.' I glanced around the room, checking up on the others. Baby and Rocky were giggling in a corner together, having seemingly made up after yesterday. Auntie and Uncle Jai were also huddled in the opposite corner, as far away from the cameras as possible, having what looked like an intriguingly serious chat. Mr Hernandez was cross-legged on the other sofa, eyes closed and chanting under his breath.

'OK,' I said. 'No one's listening.' I glanced at the nearby camera but I was pretty sure we wouldn't be heard if we kept our voices low.

'So, what's going on then?' Geena repeated.

I repeated my conversation with Dad, word for word.

'Well, if Dad wasn't at work, where was he then?' Jazz demanded.

I remembered what Baby had said. 'Do you think maybe Dad *has* got a girlfriend?' I asked hesitantly, much as I didn't like to even *say* the words.

'No,' said Geena and Jazz together.

'Why not?' Kim asked.

'Because—' I couldn't think of anything to say. Neither could Geena or Jazz.

'He's been on his own for a while now,' Kim went on quietly. 'People *do* get married again.'

'Not *Dad*,' said Jazz defiantly.

'Why not?'

'Well – because he's *Dad*,' Geena snapped.

'And why would he keep it a secret?' I glared at Kim, even though it wasn't her fault at all.

'I can think of lots of reasons,' Kim said. 'He might not want to upset you. Or maybe he wants to get to know her better before he introduces you. Or maybe he's just interested in someone and hasn't actually gone out with them yet. Or maybe—'

'Maybe you'd better shut up,' I said coldly. Kim's reasonable take on this situation was worrying me. I didn't feel reasonable about this *at all*. 'Right, the next thing to do, obviously,' I went on, glancing at Geena and Jazz, 'is to find out what's going on.'

'It might be better to wait till we get out of here,' said Kim. I ignored her until she pointed at the camera, and then I realized that I'd completely forgotten to keep my voice down during the conversation. So had Geena and Jazz.

'All these secrets are beginning to get me down,' Jazz grumbled. 'And what's going on with Auntie and Uncle Jai and the phantom honeymoon?'

'We probably shouldn't be discussing that,' Kim began, glancing at the camera.

'I don't know, but I intend to find out,' I replied, lowering my voice again and pretending Kim wasn't there.

'Is it any of your business?' asked Kim.

'I agree with Jazz,' said Geena, also pretending that Kim was invisible. 'All this is getting on my nerves.'

Jazz eyeballed Geena intently. 'Oh, and *you've* got *no* secrets at all, I suppose.'

Which was more or less what I'd been going to say.

'Me!' Geena flushed to the very tips of her ears. 'What have *I* got to do with this?'

'Jazz and I are quite frustrated that we haven't found out any more about your secret boyfriend—' I began.

'Don't start that again!' Geena whispered with a sideways glance at Dad and Auntie. Dad was still hovering in the kitchen, tidying the cupboards, and Auntie was too intent on her conversation/argument with Uncle Jai to notice anything. 'There *is* no secret boyfriend!'

'*Former* secret boyfriend then?' Jazz enquired hopefully.

Geena got up and stalked over to a corner of the room. We were running out of corners now, and only had one left if someone else had a hissy fit.

'Was that *really* necessary?' asked Kim primly.

I didn't bother to answer her. 'Jazz, our standards are slipping,' I said. 'We're no closer to finding out what Geena's been up to than we were before.'

'Goodness me, what busy little bees you are,' Kim said with weighty sarcasm. 'All these mysteries to solve!'

'Kim, go and sit in the last remaining corner before I'm forced to silence you by whatever means possible,' I advised.

Kim pulled a face at me. 'I'm the voice of your conscience, Amber,' she said solemnly. 'You know, like Jiminy Cricket in *Pinocchio*.'

Jazz burst out laughing at this, and neither Kim nor I could help smiling. Kim does get on my nerves, but she's always there for me. Bless her.

Not that I was going to take the *slightest* notice of *anything* she said.

The day crept on. At 11.30 I decided that I would only look at the clock every half-hour. When I judged that thirty minutes had dragged past, I glanced at it again. It was 11.39.

Auntie and Uncle Jai were still deep in discussion, and hadn't spoken a word to anyone else all morning. Everyone was dying to know what they were talking about but we just couldn't ask. Baby had other ideas, though.

'So, *are* you two going to Australia on honeymoon or aren't you?' Baby demanded at 11.42 precisely.

'We haven't decided yet,' Auntie snapped.

'It costs a *lot of money* to go to Australia,' Rocky remarked with a meaningful look in Baby's direction.

'What's *that* supposed to mean?' Baby asked coldly.

'Exactly what I said,' Rocky retorted.

'You're going on about that money again, aren't you?' Baby slapped him quite hard on the arm. 'I've never had such a mean and selfish boyfriend!'

'Oh, just pay him back, *please*,' Jazz groaned.

'What about your parents, Baby?' I asked.

'What!' Baby whirled round and directed a scorching stare right at me. 'What *about* my parents? What do you mean?'

I was taken aback by her reaction. 'I just meant that, if you've overspent your allowance, why don't you ask them for the money to pay Rocky back when we get out of here?'

'Oh.' Baby subsided, looking sullen. 'I see.'

'That's a great idea,' Rocky said eagerly.

'Oh, shut up!' Baby snapped. She flounced off to the other side of the room, leaving Rocky glaring after her. This was very strange. It seemed like whatever secret Baby was hiding, it definitely involved Uncle Dave and Auntie Rita too . . .

We spent the afternoon trying to guess Mr Hernandez's first name. The other teachers called him 'Ed', which we discovered was short for Eduardo, his middle name. Mr Hernandez didn't use his first name because, according to him, it was utterly vile and repulsive. So Jazz, in particular, was determined to find out exactly what it was. She started going through the alphabet, thinking up the most outlandish names possible, and had got up to G – Gustave, Godfrey, Granville – by the time we went to bed. Oh well, it passed the time a bit, I suppose.

I thought about trying another escape attempt, but with the security cameras in the corridor, it didn't seem worth it. Also it had occurred to me that I had no way of proving to Mr Gill that I'd got out, unless I gave myself up to Gareth. Scary. And I realized that there was no way George Botley was going to get in, not with CCTV everywhere and someone on guard outside the main doors.

Mr Gill's one thousand pounds was a lost cause.

Besides, I had lots to think about before I went to sleep. Maybe Geena was a lost cause, but there was Baby's extraordinary behaviour, for a start.

Auntie and Uncle Jai's on-off honeymoon.

And the one that was worrying me the most.

Dad . . .

Wednesday. We were woken up the next morning at eight o'clock by Mr Grimwade bellowing out instructions once again. This time, at least, he allowed us to shower and have breakfast before our daily challenge.

I was first into the common room. Dad was in the kitchen, making tea.

He looked slightly sheepish, but pretended to be tremendously busy.

'I thought it was Baby and Mr Hernandez's turn to make breakfast,' I said with an almighty yawn.

Dad shrugged. 'Well, I was up early, so . . .'

Guilty conscience, maybe?

'Dad, about what you said yesterday . . .' I began. 'Where were you *really* when you told us you were at work?'

I didn't mean to come right out with it, but I couldn't help myself. I *could not* be fair and logical and reasonable if – and it was still a big *if* – Dad was starting to date again. The implications were just too huge for me, Geena and Jazz. Was that selfish? Yes. But, like I said, I couldn't help it.

Dad looked very uncomfortable. 'Well, I—' Suddenly his voice changed. 'Morning, Kim! Tea's just made.'

'Oh, thanks,' Kim yawned, wandering into the common room.

Dad's obvious relief was worrying. Grabbing the tray of tea, he almost ran back to the guys' bedroom.

'Blast,' I said under my breath.

'What's going on?' asked Kim. I swear that girl has been taking lessons in interfering from the master herself, Auntie.

'Nothing.'

'Have you been hassling your dad?' Kim said sternly, and nodded pointedly at the cameras.

Oh dear.

You know, I'd completely forgotten about the cameras and hadn't even bothered to keep my voice down. Now, for the first time, I understood why people in those silly TV shows couldn't control themselves. Because they just didn't even remember the cameras were *there*. I hadn't realized before just what iron self-control Molly

Mahal had shown, never letting her mask slip, not even for a moment.

'Oh, well,' I muttered, 'I don't think anyone's going to be *that* interested.'

Anyway, maybe everyone in the school had forgotten about us by now. There might be hardly anyone watching the daily updates. Now that we'd been locked up for more than two days, it was quite difficult to remember what all the excitement had been about . . .

'You've got to stop this, Amber.'

'What?'

'Poking and prying,' Kim replied promptly. 'You're annoying your family, and you *do* have to carry on living with them when you get out of here, you know.'

'I know that.' I shrugged. 'It's just that I can't help it. It's not like I've got anything else to do at the moment. And anyway . . .' I lowered my voice. 'I don't suppose anyone outside has noticed anything, really.'

How wrong could I be? After breakfast Mr Grimwade announced that Dad and Uncle Jai were to go to the end of the corridor, where the next challenge would be waiting for us. They hurried off, leaving us in a state of high excitement, and when they came back . . .

'It's a karaoke machine!' Mr Hernandez announced gleefully. 'Great!'

My heart dropped. Singing is *not* one of my strong points. Oh, well, maybe I'd be awarded points for comedy value . . .

'There's something else.' Uncle Jai took a white envelope from the pocket of his jeans and opened it. *'Song suggestions for the contestants,'* he read out. He cleared his throat. *'Baby* – Money, Money, Money *by Abba.'*

'What!' Baby screamed furiously. 'That's just not funny!'

'Good choice,' said Rocky with a smirk.

'Mr and Mrs Arora . . .' Uncle Jai's voice faltered a bit. 'Australia *by the Manic Street Preachers . . .'*

'How utterly non-amusing,' said Auntie frostily.

'Can I see?' I asked, taking the list. Now, too late, I realized that the sixth-formers, at least, *had* been listening to what we were saying, and they were now using it to spice up the action . . .

'Don't tell me what mine is,' Geena muttered.

I scanned the paper. 'Yours is *Once I Had a Secret Love* from the musical *Calamity Jane.'*

Geena turned quite pale. 'That's not true,' she said, glancing at Auntie and Dad.

'I hope not,' Dad replied sternly.

'And Dad's is *Crazy in Love* by Beyoncé.'

'Ah.' Dad looked supremely uncomfortable.

'Look at yours, Amber.' Kim pointed at the list over my shoulder. '*Do You Want to Know a Secret?* by the Beatles.'

Geena, Dad, Auntie, Uncle Jai and Baby all turned to glare at me at the exact same moment.

'Mine is *I Predict a Riot* by the Kaiser Chiefs,' Kim went on. 'And I think that's a pretty good choice, actually.'

Not surprisingly, none of us except Kim chose the songs that had been suggested. Oh, and Mr Hernandez, whose performance of the sixties classic, *Wild Thing*, complete with Austin Powers-type dancing, must have won him a few more votes.

I was almost afraid to say anything to *anyone* that afternoon. And no one else was talking much either. Jazz was still trying to guess Mr Hernandez's first name and was up to M – Murdoch, Mingus, Marcellus – but that was all. Auntie and Uncle Jai were barely speaking; neither were Rocky and Baby. Dad looked permanently worried; so did Geena.

There was such tension in the air, it was almost unbearable. How the people on TV could stand to be locked up for weeks on end, I just didn't know. We only had two more days to go and I was ready to punch my way through a brick wall to get out of there.

I had to keep reminding myself *why* we were doing this.

To make money to donate to the school in order to get the library named after Mum . . .

But what had seemed such a completely fab idea at the time was rapidly turning into something of an ordeal.

Oh, and there was more to come.

Thursday.

Now I really *was* counting down the minutes until we got out of here at five the following day. I was secretly starting to wish I'd listened to Auntie and Kim before now. Not that I'd told them that, of course. But they were right. I wouldn't be asking any more nosy questions. Whatever family secrets were waiting to be uncovered, they shouldn't be exposed to everyone in the school.

Well, that's what I thought, anyway.

Some people had other ideas.

At eleven Rocky and Mr Hernandez were ordered to go to the corridor to collect the next challenge. They came in carrying a cardboard box covered in red foil. It had gold cut-out letters on the side which read TRUTH OR DARE?

I instantly felt a bit anxious as Mr Hernandez opened the envelope. What was this all about?

'*Sit in a circle,*' Mr Hernandez read out. '*Everyone must draw a slip of paper in turn until the box is empty. The paper will say "Truth" or "Dare". The person sitting on their left must then either set a dare or ask a question. The question must be answered truthfully.*'

'This sounds like a ridiculous game,' Auntie commented tartly as we gathered in a circle. 'What *is* Mr Grimwade thinking?'

'I'll be having a few words with him when I get out,' Uncle Jai muttered, looking highly annoyed.

I didn't say anything but I guessed that this had been thought up by the sixth-formers. And that it was something to do with Gareth Parker, although I did not know what.

The first person to plunge her hand into the box was Baby.

'*Truth,*' she read out, and stared aggressively at Rocky, who was sitting on her left.

'OK, why won't you ask your parents for the money to pay me back?' Rocky asked promptly.

Baby's face dropped. Suddenly, and without warning, she broke into noisy sobs.

'Oh, my dear,' said Auntie anxiously. 'What's the matter?'

'We haven't *got* any money!' Baby gulped.

'Don't be daft,' I said. 'You're loaded . . .'

'Not any more,' sobbed Baby.

We all stared at her in bemusement.

'The business is doing really badly and Mum and Dad have gone to India to try and borrow some money from relatives,' Baby wept. 'But they told me they aren't having any luck so far. We're going to be p-p-poor, just like you!'

We stared at her, transfixed. So *that* was what this had all been about. I guessed now that the conversation I'd overheard on the day of the slave duties was Baby talking to her parents. And that it had been her mum or dad who'd called her on the day of the contest.

'So how are you going to pay me back then?' Rocky demanded.

'Rocky!' Uncle Jai said sternly.

'Sorry – I meant, bad luck, Babe.' Looking a bit sheepish, Rocky patted Baby on the arm.

'Well, you'll be all right, won't you, Baby?' Jazz said kindly. 'I mean, you've got enough designer clothes to last until you're about seventy years old.'

But Baby shook her head violently. 'You don't understand,' she wailed. 'We might have to move out of our house too.'

Auntie got up, gave Baby a hug and handed her a tissue.

'I think we should stop this game right now,' Dad said.

'So do I,' Uncle Jai agreed.

'No, I want to get the chance to ask a question!' Gulping, Baby dried her tears and thrust the box at Rocky. He got a 'Dare' and was challenged by Mr Hernandez to do a yoga pose called The Crow. This involved squatting and lifting your feet off the floor, supporting yourself on your hands. Rocky failed badly and ended up bumping his head on the floor, which he complained loudly about.

The next sensation occurred when Auntie drew 'Truth'. Jazz, who was on her left, immediately jumped straight in.

'Are you and Uncle Jai going to Australia?' she asked curiously.

'We haven't decided yet,' Auntie said in a clipped voice. Uncle Jai looked *very* uncomfortable.

I stared at them both, and suddenly something clicked.

'You're not – you're not thinking of *moving* there, are you?' I blurted out.

Silence.

'I think that's *two* questions, Amber,' said Mr Hernandez.

'Of course they're not moving,' Jazz said robustly. 'Why would they?'

Auntie and Uncle Jai both stared down at their feet.

'Well, *are* you?' Geena asked in a supremely shocked voice. From the expression on Dad's face, I could see that he hadn't known anything about this either.

Auntie and Uncle Jai glanced at each other. Auntie cleared her throat.

'It's just that – well, your uncle has been offered a job—'

'A very good job,' Uncle Jai cut in.

'By a friend of his who lives in Sydney.' Auntie still couldn't look us in the eye.

'Australia's so far away!' Jazz gasped. 'Miles and miles and miles . . .'

'Yes, Jasvinder,' Auntie said edgily. 'I know.'

'But you *can't* go,' Jazz insisted.

Auntie bit her lip but said nothing. Uncle Jai looked pretty wretched too. I guessed that the stress of trying to make this difficult decision was the reason why they'd been behaving a bit oddly for the last month or so.

'We'd miss you both like mad,' I added, and Geena nodded. All right, so it was emotional blackmail, but it was *true*.

'Girls,' Dad said, 'this has to be your aunt and uncle's decision.' But he sounded quite miserable himself.

'An interesting place, Australia,' Mr Hernandez remarked. 'There are a lot of kangaroos there.'

'So we've been told,' Auntie said quietly. 'And when we've decided what we're going to do, you girls and your dad will be the first to know.'

'And Mr Morgan,' Uncle Jai added with a nervous look at the cameras.

Well, how could we concentrate on the game properly after *that* bombshell? Especially with the whole Baby thing going on too. The level of tension in the room had rocketed as we once again went through the motions of playing Truth or Dare. But I was certain almost everyone had something else on their mind.

Dad, Geena, Kim and Mr Hernandez got 'Dares', and Geena and Dad looked mightily relieved. I was so intent on thinking about all the implications of Auntie and Uncle Jai moving to Australia, though, that I wasn't really concentrating. Until I put my hand in the box and pulled out 'Truth'.

'Oh, great!' said Baby eagerly. 'Now I get to ask the question! So, Amber, *do* you secretly fancy that boy who's always hanging round you? What's his name? George Bottomley?'

'Botley,' I said, feeling suddenly hot all over. It seemed like everyone's eyes were boring into me at once. 'Well . . .' What *was* the truth? I hardly knew myself. 'I suppose I *do* like him, in a way – but just as a friend. Sort of.'

'Oh.' Baby looked disappointed. 'I thought you might have something you wanted to share with us.'

'No,' I said firmly. Of course I *did* have a secret but it was nothing to do with George Botley. All would be revealed tomorrow when the contest was over. Or not. It all depended on *one* person. And I didn't have much faith in that person coming through for me *at all*.

'Right, there are enough slips left for us to have another go.' Mr Hernandez peered into the box. 'Let's change places to make it more interesting.'

We all moved seats. Jazz and I both tried to get near Geena but she plonked herself down quickly between Mr Hernandez and Rocky, looking very smug. Obviously she was determined to fend off any questions about mystery boyfriends.

On the other hand, Dad was now sitting with

Baby on his left. He looked worried and he had a right to be. When he pulled out 'Truth', Baby pounced like a spider on a poor little fly.

'My question is – have you got a girlfriend, Uncle?'

Oooh! There was a sharp intake of breath around the circle.

'I don't think that's appropriate at all, Baby,' Auntie snapped.

'It's all right,' Dad said quietly. 'No, I don't have a girlfriend.'

Geena, Jazz and I glanced at each other, relief written all over us.

'However,' Dad stumbled on manfully, 'I do have a friend who is a lady. I mean, a woman. But we're just friends.'

That sounded slightly more worrying and would require more discussion later with Geena and Jazz. Meanwhile the box was making its way around the circle once again and I was relieved this time to get a 'Dare', even though Jazz dared me to sing the school song backwards. I can hardly sing *forwards*, so at least it was quite amusing and lightened the tension a little.

But the biggest shock of all came when Geena pulled out 'Truth'. She looked slightly concerned, but only slightly, as she turned to Rocky. Maybe she thought he was going to ask her if she thought his rapping was cool or something. But she was unprepared for the question he actually asked, as were we all.

'Right, then . . .' Rocky sat forward in his chair. 'So have you ever, like, been out with a boy on a secret date without your dad or auntie finding out?'

Geena turned completely pale.

'I told him to ask that when we were changing seats,' Baby said with great satisfaction.

'You may as well tell us the truth, Geena,' Auntie said grimly. 'I have a suspicion that there's been something going on.'

Jazz, in a state of high excitement, pinched my arm rather hard. I barely noticed the pain because my eyes were riveted on Geena.

'Oh all right!' Geena muttered, fidgeting uncomfortably in her seat. 'I did go out with . . . *someone* – but just twice. I finished it by telling him I didn't really like him, but it wasn't that. I just couldn't stand all the sneaking around.'

'*Who* was it?' Jazz demanded breathlessly.

Geena bit her lip. There was a tense silence which seemed to last for decades.

'Gareth Parker,' she said at last.

'GARETH PARKER!' I screamed.

Jazz fell back in her chair, stunned. Kim was goggling at Geena in disbelief. Dad, Uncle Jai, Auntie and even Mr Hernandez looked shocked. None of us could take it in.

'What, you mean that grim-looking boy who's one of the sixth-formers?' asked Auntie.

'He's very good-looking without his glasses,' Geena mumbled, eyes on the floor.

'I told you so, Amber,' Baby said triumphantly. 'Heathrow. I mean, Heathcliff.'

'Oh, *now* I see why he's been so mean,' I said slowly, working it out. 'He was getting his own back on Geena. And that must be why he bid for us all at the slave auction. He only wanted to win *you* . . .' I glanced at Geena, who was *completely* overcome with embarrassment. 'But it would have been too obvious if he'd only bid the once.'

'So he *was* staring at our house with his binoculars that time!' Jazz gasped. 'He was trying to spot Geena!'

'Is this guy a stalker or what?' asked Rocky.

'I must say, I don't like the sound of *that*,' Dad said with a frown.

'He's not a stalker,' Geena muttered. 'He wanted to talk to me and I wouldn't. That's all.'

'And it must have been Gareth who passed you

that note Baby spotted,' I guessed. 'What did it say?'

Geena turned pink. 'I can't remember,' she muttered untruthfully.

'Did you kiss him, Geena?' Jazz asked with rampant curiosity.

'Oh, really, Jazz!' Geena snarled.

'Ooh, Gareth could be watching this right now if he's on camera duty!' Jazz exclaimed, opening her eyes very wide. 'And even if he isn't, I bet he'll see it later.' Her eyes opened even wider. 'Oh! The whole *school* could be watching all this later today!'

We stared at each other in horror. We'd been so caught up in the unfolding drama that we'd all forgotten that the cameras were rolling.

'Maybe people have lost interest in the contest by now,' Geena said hopefully. 'There might be hardly anyone coming to watch the updates after school.'

'But if no one's voting, then we'll make hardly any money for our Mum Fund,' I pointed out. I didn't know which was worse – washing my family's dirty linen in public or not raising any money. It was a tough one.

'I think that all these things should be left alone until we get out of here tomorrow,' Dad said in an authoritative tone. 'We'll have *plenty* of time to discuss everything then.' He glanced at Geena, who looked apprehensive.

'What drama!' said Mr Hernandez, flopping back on the sofa. 'This is better than *Neighbours*.'

I knew what he meant. But thank goodness the game was now over. It had well and truly put a killer cat amongst the pigeons . . .

Following on from all those amazing revelations, the afternoon was supremely dull. Dad, Auntie and Uncle Jai were on guard, making sure that nothing that had come to light during the Truth or Dare game was mentioned again *at all* in front of the cameras. It was *extremely* annoying.

Drained by all the drama, we went to bed very early that night. I was hoping that Auntie would fall asleep first. There was no hope of getting any more out of her about the proposed move to Australia, but at least then Jazz and I would have a chance to quiz Geena.

I mean, *Gareth Parker!!!*

I was still in shock.

But Auntie wasn't having any of it. My eyelids insisted on closing while she was still sitting up, arms folded, waiting for the rest of us to go to sleep. Even though I was also thinking about the end of the contest tomorrow, and whether my Big

Secret would come out, I just couldn't stay awake . . .

Some time later – I don't know how much – I woke up with a jolt. The classroom was now in darkness but I could hear a steady *tap-tap-tap* sound on the door. I think that was what had woken me up.

'Rocky!' I thought. I guessed that he'd sneaked out to see Baby. Well, I'd give him the fright of his life . . .

I slipped out of bed and tiptoed over to the classroom door. But it was *me* who got the fright of my life.

I looked through the glass and saw George Botley grinning back at me.

Chapter Eleven

'George!' I gasped, wondering for a moment if I was still asleep and having a nightmare. 'What – what the hell are you *doing* here?'

'Well, that's nice,' George said in an injured tone. I could just about hear him through the door. 'You *told* me to break you out. So here I am.'

'Yes, but – but . . .' I was floundering badly. 'How did you get in?'

'I climbed through a window,' George replied.

'But there are CCTV cameras in the corridors!' I said anxiously. 'A sixth-former or a teacher will be along in a moment to throw you out!'

'No, they won't.' George sounded supremely confident for some unknown reason. 'But we've only got about ten minutes, so we've got to hurry.'

'Amber, what's going on?'

Auntie's voice behind me almost made me

jump out of my skin. I spun round and accidentally knocked a pot plant off the nearby bookcase. It crashed to the floor and smashed loudly.

A second later Auntie switched on the light. I stood there blinking, surrounded by bits of compost and leaves. Meanwhile Geena, Jazz, Kim and Baby sat up yawning and stared at me.

'What's going on?' Auntie asked again.

'HELP!' Jazz screeched, pointing at the door. 'There's a horrible ghostly face looking in at us!'

'Don't panic,' I said. 'It's only George Botley.'

'George Botley!' Auntie repeated in amazement. 'How did *he* get in? And more to the point, what's he doing here?'

'I've come to break Amber out, like she asked me to,' George called through the door. 'So she can claim Mr Gill's thousand pounds.'

Auntie turned and threw a piercing stare my way, which made me blush. 'How strange,' she said. 'Amber never mentioned to me that she'd asked for your help, George.'

'Or me,' Geena and Jazz both chimed in.

'Well, I didn't really think he'd manage it,' I muttered defensively. 'And I'm not actually convinced that it's going to work anyway. Whoever's watching the CCTV cameras tonight would have seen him come in.'

'I keep telling you,' George said impatiently, 'they won't. But we've only got about nine minutes left now.'

'What do you mean, George?' asked Auntie.

'The caretaker's on camera duty tonight,' George explained. 'But he nips out every hour to have a ciggie. He's away for ten minutes on the dot. That's why we've only got a bit of time left.'

Auntie grabbed her dressing gown and then unlocked the door.

'How do you know all this, George?' asked Geena.

George grinned. 'I've been asking around,' he replied. 'And I keep my ears open.' He raised his eyebrows. 'Nice jim-jams, Amber.'

I scowled, wishing I'd brought some other nightwear instead of my cosy, candy-pink PJs covered with fluffy white bunnies.

'There must be other people – teachers or sixth-formers – patrolling around the block tonight,' I said tartly. 'How are we going to avoid *them*?'

George shrugged. 'We'll just have to keep a look out,' he said. 'Are you up for this or not, Amber?'

'*I* am, definitely!' Jazz cut in, scrambling for her slippers.

'Only one of us needs to go . . .' I began.

'Why don't we *all* go?' Kim suggested. 'Mr Gill might give you a bit of extra money then, Amber.'

'I'm not going if it's cold outside,' Baby grumbled.

'Don't worry.' George winked at her. 'You're hot enough to keep yourself warm.'

Baby giggled.

'George,' I said coldly, 'this is no time for flirting.'

'We'll *all* go,' said Auntie. 'Then I can keep an eye on everyone. Lead on, George.'

We all hurried out into the moonlit corridor behind George. As we did so, a tall thin shadow loomed over us on the opposite wall.

'It's a ghost!' Baby screamed.

'What's going on?' Dad stepped out of the dark common room, looking bewildered. 'We heard a crash and it woke us up.' He looked even more confused when he spotted George. 'And what's *he* doing here?'

'No time to explain, Dad,' I said hastily. 'We're off to claim Mr Gill's thousand pounds.'

'Can we come too?' Mr Hernandez rushed out of the common room, wearing eye-popping lime-green pyjamas. He was followed closely by Uncle Jai. 'This is a bit of an adventure!'

'Where's Rocky?' asked Baby.

'He's still asleep,' Uncle Jai replied.

We all tiptoed off down the corridor in a long line towards the window where George had let himself in. After a moment or two we heard footsteps and Rocky joined us.

'Why did you leave me on my own?' he complained to the other guys. 'You know I don't like the dark!'

Baby sniggered.

'Here we are.' George stopped underneath the same window I'd tried to escape through three days earlier. 'Want a leg-up, Amber?'

'No, thank you, George.' Dad had already heaved me up and I was climbing through. Geena and Kim followed me outside.

'It's freezing,' Baby moaned as she joined us.

A few minutes later we were all out. After being locked up for four days, it felt wonderful to be out in the cool night air.

'I've brought my camera.' George whipped a dinky little digital camera out of his pocket. 'And a copy of today's newspaper so we can see the date. That's how they do it in the movies.'

'You've thought of everything, George,' said Auntie. 'Well done. But I'm sure you shouldn't be out this late, you know. It's well after midnight. Does your mum know?'

'Oh, my mum brought me here,' George explained cheerfully as we all lined up for the photo. 'She's waiting in the car at the playground gates. She thinks it's a great laugh. You know, she's a bit mad like that.'

Yes, that probably summed up Mrs Botley only too well. You'd have to be slightly off-the-wall to produce a son like George.

George shoved the newspaper at me and I held it up. Then he snapped away several times as we did all the silly things people usually do in group pictures, like thumbs-ups and rabbit-ears. Then, when we'd checked that the photos had turned out OK, we tiptoed over to the window.

'So what's happening in school then, George?' I asked curiously. 'Is everyone watching us, or have they lost interest by now?'

'Oh, I can't tell you that,' George said in a most infuriating manner. 'It's against the rules.'

I ground my teeth. 'Can't you give me *some* idea? Especially after what happened today?'

'Oh, you mean the Truth or Dare game?' George chuckled and winked at me. 'Thanks for saying you liked me.'

'As a *friend*,' I reminded him, with as much dignity as I could muster in my fluffy bunny PJs.

George shrugged. 'It's a start,' he replied

jauntily. 'Yeah, that Truth or Dare bit was gripping. Edge-of-the-seat stuff.'

'Yes, but exactly *how* many people were on the edge of their seats?' I asked urgently. 'Two? Ten? Thirty? Two hundred?'

George cocked his head to one side and regarded me thoughtfully. 'What do you want me to say, Amber?' he asked as we reached the window. 'I *could* tell you that there were only about five of us watching the update after school today.'

I felt a mix of relief and disappointment. 'And would that be true?'

'Or,' George went on, ignoring my question, 'I could tell you that almost the whole school was there. And that lots of the kids' parents have started popping in to watch too, and bringing their friends, because everyone's really hooked on seeing what happens next. And that *loads* of people are voting every single day.'

I stared at him in amazement. 'And would *that* be true?'

George winked at me again. 'What do *you* think, Amber? See you tomorrow afternoon when you get out.' He slapped me on the back in an annoyingly matey manner and ran off. I stared after him as Dad and Uncle Jai pulled the window wide open again. Could it really be true? Had the contest been a huge success?

'Me first!' Baby elbowed Kim and Jazz aside. 'I'm cold.'

Dad and Uncle Jai bent down to give Baby a leg-up. As they did so, someone with a torch came round from the front of the building.

It was Gareth Parker.

There was a moment of completely incredulous silence. I don't think Gareth could believe his eyes either as he played the torch slowly over all of us. At last the beam came to rest on Geena and she flushed bright red.

Oh, this was *so* unfair! I swallowed hard, anxiety overwhelming me. We'd *all* broken the rules. What if the contest was cancelled and we had to give the money back or something like that? All our hard work would be wasted.

'I suppose it's no use asking you not to tell on us?' I muttered.

Looking highly embarrassed, Gareth cleared his throat. 'Go on,' he said gruffly.

'What?' I asked, confused.

'Go on, climb through the window,' he muttered. 'I haven't seen you.'

'You mean – you're letting us go?' Jazz squeaked. 'You're not going to tell anyone?'

Gareth shook his head. I glanced at Geena, whose face was now literally on fire.

'Oh, come on, what are we waiting for?' Baby said impatiently. She shot a brilliant smile at Gareth and then launched herself at Dad and Uncle Jai. They hadn't quite braced themselves, and staggered backwards. Baby climbed all over them and pushed herself through the window back into the corridor.

'I'll see you later,' Gareth mumbled, backing away. He was speaking to everyone but looking at Geena.

'Gareth, wait!'

As he rushed off back round the front of the block again, I ran after him. I'd just realized that Gareth was someone who could help me with my Secret Plan.

'What is it, Amber?' He came to a halt, looking flustered.

'I just wanted to say thanks.' I beamed at him. 'Oh, and this . . .' I reached up and whispered in his ear.

'You – what do you mean, Amber?' Gareth's mouth dropped right open and he goggled at me. 'You can't be serious! That's just *not* going to happen, is it?'

'I don't know,' I said with a shrug. 'But will you

put the word around, just in case? I promise I'll take the blame if it all gets messy.'

Gareth hesitated for a minute. Then he nodded.

'All right,' he said. 'But I think you're crazy.'

'Yes, and it runs in the family, you know,' I replied. 'Geena's a complete nutcase too.'

Gareth blushed as red as a rose.

'Are you being nice to us tonight because you heard Geena say in the Truth or Dare game that she liked you really?' I asked curiously.

'See you tomorrow, Amber,' was all Gareth said as he strode off.

The others were already inside and Dad and Uncle Jai were waiting to lift me through the window.

'What was all *that* about?' asked Dad.

'Oh, nothing much,' I replied. I wasn't about to give up my secret just yet.

Geena looked at me suspiciously as I climbed in. 'What did you run after Gareth for?' she asked.

'Oh, don't be so paranoid,' I said. 'It was nothing to do with you. Just a little surprise for tomorrow.'

'I think we've had enough surprises for tonight,' Auntie said with a great yawn. 'Back to bed, everyone.'

'Oh, yes, I must get my beauty sleep,' Baby

exclaimed. 'After all, as the winner of the contest, I'm going to be interviewed by the TV company tomorrow.'

Jazz scowled at her.

'Bed!' Auntie ordered, hustling us into our classroom.

So now we had Mr Gill's money to add to our total, I thought as I snuggled down in my camp bed. Then, if what George Botley had hinted at was true, we might also have made a lot of money from all the votes. Could we possibly get near our target?

And tomorrow, when we were finally released, could be the best day of all, if only my plan worked out. Then everyone would know *my* secret.

'Fingers crossed,' I whispered.

Because, sadly, I was very afraid that my Big Secret was going to turn out to be a Very Big Disaster.

'So, what have I learned from my experiences this week?' Baby said, flinging her arms wide in a melodramatic gesture. 'Oh, lots and lots!'

It was Friday. The clock was ticking towards midday and we were gathered in the common room for the final challenge. Mr Grimwade had told us that we had to sum up our experience of the last five days in just a few sentences. Tricky, really, considering how much emotional drama we'd lived through.

Kim, Jazz, Mr Hernandez and Rocky had all had a turn so far. Kim and Jazz had both gone on – a touch offensively, I felt – about how no one but 'a single-minded lunatic' like Amber could have planned all this and then gone ahead and done it. I liked the compliments but could have done without the constant emphasis on how crazy I was. Mr Hernandez had also said almost the same thing – which was rich, coming from him. Rocky had simply moaned about how being locked up 'stifled his creativity'. Which was lucky as it meant we hadn't been forced to listen to his rapping for hours on end.

'I've learned that money isn't *everything*,' Baby went on, directing a stern glance in Rocky's direction. 'I just think that I've been a teeny-weeny bit selfish, expecting my mum and dad to earn all the money. If we're going to be poor from now on, I want to help. So, as soon as I get out of here, I'm going to look for a job so that I can contribute to the family budget!'

We burst into spontaneous applause. I could hardly see Baby teetering through a newspaper round on her high heels, but obviously she'd had plenty of time to think while we'd been holed up for the last five days. I actually felt rather proud of her.

'What are you going to *do*, though, Baby?' asked Auntie, obviously having the same thoughts about newspaper rounds and high heels as I'd had myself.

'I'm going to act in Bollywood films!' Baby declared. 'I'm sure I'll be a big success!'

Oh well, it was the thought that counted.

'Me next.' Geena stood up, looking anxious to get it over with. 'I just wanted to say that I agree with what Kim and Jazz said about Amber being totally mad. I never, ever thought this contest would work.'

'I think everyone gets that I'm a raving loon by now,' I said.

'But I also wanted to say – well, I'm totally fed up with secrets and I'm sorry, I'll never do anything behind your backs again,' Geena rushed on, glancing from Dad to Auntie.

'Yeah, right,' Jazz whispered to me, a little too loudly.

'I'd like to speak for both myself and my wife.' Uncle Jai stood up as Geena, fiery-faced, sat down in her chair. 'We've decided that we're going to turn down the job in Australia.'

There were gasps and cheers, and Geena, Jazz and I rushed over to give Auntie and Uncle a big hug.

'You've made the right decision,' said Jazz happily. 'Think how boring your lives would be without us.'

'Yes, how could we leave behind someone as crazy as Amber?' Auntie added, looking radiant with relief. 'She obviously needs us all to look after her, or who knows what mad schemes she'll come up with next?'

'I'll ignore that bit,' I said with a grin that stretched from one ear to the other. 'I'm *so* glad you're staying.'

'Me too,' said Dad. 'Well, it's my turn now. Where do I start? I was also one of the many people who thought this would never work. But I didn't count on having quite such enterprising daughters.' He smiled at me. 'Especially Amber.'

I smiled back at him.

'It's quite scary to think what she might be when she grows up,' Dad went on teasingly. 'Prime Minister, maybe? But I'm very proud of all my girls. And I know their mum would be too.'

Oh dear. That had almost done for me. With a gulp, I stood up. It was my turn.

'OK, I'm going to admit it now,' I said. 'I didn't think this would work either. All right, it was my crazy idea but I couldn't have done it without all of you taking part. I always knew I had a fantastic family and good friends, and you've proved it. Thank you. I honestly don't care who wins. I just hope that Mum can see us now, and if she can, I hope she's proud of me too. That's all.'

I glanced around. There was hardly a dry eye in the house, apart from Rocky, who was biting his nails, looking bored.

Then I wondered if I should tell them my secret. But I simply didn't get a chance.

'A very moving speech, Amber,' Mr Grimwade said over the loudspeaker, sounding quite affected himself, bless. *'Thank you, contestants. It is now twelve o'clock, and you may switch the cameras off.'*

Uncle Jai and Mr Hernandez got up. Seeing those little green lights go off was a huge relief, I can tell you.

'We will see you all at five after the last update session has taken place, and all today's votes have been collected in,' Mr Grimwade added. And then there was silence.

'Oh, goodie!' Jazz sighed, slumping back onto the sofa. *'Now* we can find out all the goss that we weren't allowed to talk about when we were being filmed.' She eyeballed Geena. 'Like Gareth Parker, for instance.'

'That's enough, Jasvinder,' Auntie cut in smoothly.

There was a tap at the common room door. Uncle Jai went to open it, and outside stood Gareth Parker himself, along with Soo-Lin, both carrying plastic crates.

'We've brought your stuff back,' Gareth muttered, trying not to look at Geena but unable to help himself.

'Thank you,' Dad said quite sternly. He and Uncle Jai took the crates and ushered Gareth and Soo-Lin out without another word. Geena studiously did not look at me and Jazz.

'She won't be able to avoid us when we get home, though, will she?' Jazz whispered in my ear.

The crates contained our mobiles and iPods and all the bits and pieces we'd given up when the contest started, and we fell on them with glee. I grabbed my mobile, wondering if I would have any messages from the one person I was hoping would contact me. But there weren't any. There were texts from Kiran and Chelsea and Sharelle and some of my other friends, saying that they'd be waiting to see me when I got out and wishing me luck. Nothing else. I was now starting to feel rather anxious as I realized what *might* be waiting for me when I finally got out. Seriously, I could be in huge trouble.

Five o'clock. We'd been told to leave the common room and wait at the main doors. By now I was feeling sick with nerves. I didn't care who won. I just wanted to get out there and find out what was going on.

'Are you all right, Amber?' Auntie asked, staring at me closely.

'Fine,' I replied, and tried to smile but my mouth just wouldn't co-operate.

'*Contestants!*' Mr Grimwade boomed over the loudspeaker. '*I shall now announce the results in reverse order. Please make your way to the front of the main school building after leaving the sixth-form block.*'

'Ooh, this is it!' Baby proclaimed, primping her curls. 'I hope they tell us how many votes we've each got. I bet I beat all you suckers by miles!'

'I'm going to be *really* annoyed if she wins,' Jazz grumbled in my ear.

'*First*' – Mr Grimwade paused dramatically and I gritted my teeth with tension – '*Rocky Gill!*'

'Hey!' Rocky looked supremely pleased with himself. 'I won!'

'It's reverse order, you idiot.' Baby giggled, shoving him towards the door.

Rocky looked outraged. 'You mean I'm *last*?' he gasped. 'It's a fix!'

The door was swung open from outside as if by magic and Rocky stomped out. Then the door closed behind him.

'Ha ha, I *knew* he wouldn't win,' Baby said with immense satisfaction. 'He was so mean to me about that money.'

'Next – Baby Ahluwahlia!'

'No way!' Baby screeched indignantly. 'I demand a recount!'

As the door opened, she pushed it viciously back and we heard a muffled *'Ow!'* from the other side of it.

Baby was followed by Dad, then Kim. They each gave me a hug before the doors opened and they left. It was December so it was dark outside by now, but there seemed to be lots of light coming from the main school building. As the doors swung shut behind Dad, I could hear a lot of noise coming from the playground and I wondered how many people were there waiting for us. It could be a bit embarrassing if there were only, say, ten. But it didn't sound like it. I was beginning to think that George had told me the truth when he said that the whole school *and* people from outside were hooked on the contest. I'd done what I'd set out to do. How amazing. But, very possibly, I was now about to ruin everything . . .

'*And next to leave,*' Mr Grimwade announced, '*is Jasvinder Dhillon.*'

'What!' Jazz looked gobsmacked. 'You mean, I didn't even beat Mr Hernandez?'

'Yes, I find that quite strange too,' Mr Hernandez agreed.

'Tell me your first name before I leave, sir,' Jazz begged as the door swung open.

'It's James,' Mr Hernandez replied promptly.

'*James!*' Jazz screeched. 'But you said it was vile and repulsive!'

'And so it is,' said Mr Hernandez cheerily. 'I'm not a James-type person at all.'

Looking defeated, Jazz trudged outside.

Then Mr Hernandez was announced and, still looking cheerful, he left after shaking my hand very solemnly.

The next result was a surprise – a tie between Geena and Uncle Jai. They went out together, leaving me and Auntie alone. I was so nervous by now, I could barely swallow.

'I hope you win, Amber,' said Auntie. 'You

seriously do deserve it, my dear. But I wish you'd tell me what's bothering you.'

I needed to tell *someone*.

'Well, it's like this—' I began. But Mr Grimwade was back.

'*And second place goes to Mrs Arora!*'

Auntie gave me a quick hug, looking very pleased. 'Congratulations, Amber! You've won. Now, what were you going to tell me?'

But the doors were already swinging open.

'It's all right,' I replied. 'Go on, you'll find out soon anyway, one way or another.'

Auntie looked a little worried but did as I said. After she'd gone, I paced up and down, wondering what was going to happen now.

Suddenly the door opened again and Mr Grimwade, Gareth and Soo-Lin came in.

'Congratulations, Amber!' Mr Grimwade beamed at me and shook my hand very enthusiastically. 'Follow me. I think you're going to be *very* surprised!'

'In a good way?' I asked apprehensively.

Mr Grimwade did not reply. As I followed him out of the sixth-form block, I hung back for a moment.

'Did you do what I asked you to?' I whispered to Gareth.

He nodded. But he looked extremely nervous too, which didn't reassure me in the slightest.

'And did it work?' I asked in a low voice.

'See for yourself,' Gareth replied as we crossed over to the main playground.

As we rounded the corner, I was met by a wall of noise and light that almost deafened and blinded me. The playground was literally crammed with people, who began applauding the minute they set eyes on me. There were more bystanders lined up and down the street outside the playground gates, stopping the traffic. The police were there and they'd set up barriers to stop the crowds surging forward. Cameras flashed. Cheers echoed in my ears. I could see the local news crew and several other TV vans, including one from the BBC. Dazed, I wondered if I was asleep and having a dream. Which might very easily turn into a nightmare. Where had all these people come from?

'The contest has proved *very* popular, Amber,' Mr Grimwade said with satisfaction. 'We've had such big audiences coming to the screenings – pupils *and* parents, as well as people from the local businesses who've donated money – that we've had to run the film twice the last few days, to fit everyone in! You've raised a lot of cash, my dear. Well done.'

'Thanks,' I managed to say. But I knew that all these people weren't here simply because of the contest. I'd asked Gareth to do something for me, he'd done it and this was the result.

'This way, Amber.' Mr Grimwade took my arm and led me over to a small platform that had been set up in front of the school doors. Mr Morgan was waiting there. So were Dad, Kim, Geena, Jazz and the others. They looked as dazed as I felt.

'Amber, what *have* you been up to?' Auntie asked as I stumbled over to join them. 'Why are all these people here?'

I did say something but nobody heard me because, suddenly, the noise intensified. There were gasps and more cheers and whoops, a Mexican wave of noise that began in the street and rolled towards us as we stood in the playground.

I saw a white limousine making its way slowly towards the playground gates. There the car purred to a halt and the police sprang forward to hold back the crowds.

The door of the limousine swung open.

Out stepped Molly Mahal.

Chapter Twelve

She'd come.

I'd written to Molly to ask her to visit today at five o'clock when our contest ended. I'd even asked Gareth Parker to start the rumours that she'd be here to congratulate the winner. That was why so many people had turned up.

However, I'd never really allowed myself to believe that Molly *would* come. She hadn't replied to my invitation before the contest.

But she was here.

'Amber!' Jazz grabbed my arm, disbelief written all over her face. '*How?*'

'I asked her,' I replied. I did not say that I'd written to Molly almost every single day since *Who's in the House?* had ended, asking – begging – her to come. That would stay my little secret.

Molly had stopped by the playground gates,

the two burly minders on either side of her dwarfing everyone, even the police. Stunning in a sapphire-blue sari and matching high heels, she was signing autographs. Mrs Openshaw, the cook, was one of the lucky recipients, I noted.

'But – but – but . . .' Kim was opening and shutting her mouth but not much was coming out of it.

'Molly – *here*?' Geena looked utterly bewildered. 'But she's such a big star now!'

Molly Mahal was making her way through the crowd, which parted smoothly for her on either side. She moved directly over to the platform, where a stunned Mr Grimwade and Mr Morgan were standing with their mouths quite literally agape.

'Hello, Amber,' said Molly, looking up at me. She was so composed, you'd have thought I'd only seen her yesterday instead of seven or eight months ago.

'Oh – ah – hello,' I managed.

The minders assisted her onto the platform, where, with supreme self-confidence, she smiled at Mr Morgan and whisked the microphone from his hand. Cameras flashed and hundreds of mobile phones were held aloft to capture her picture as she stepped forward.

'Dear friends, I'm so glad to be back with you here at Coppergate School.' Molly waved and nodded graciously, waiting for the applause to subside. 'But today isn't really about me at all. As many of you will know, Amber and her sisters have been raising money for the school in order to have the library named after their late mother.'

One of the minders passed Molly an envelope.

'I'm therefore delighted to say that Picture This, the TV company who make *Who's in the House?*, would like to make a generous donation to the girls' fund,' Molly went on.

She held out the envelope towards me. Auntie gave me a little push and I stumbled forward, almost blinded by the cameras flashing again. My hands were shaking so much, it took me ages to open the envelope, and I was shocked to see that the cheque was for fifteen hundred pounds.

'Smile, Amber,' Molly whispered, turning me slightly sideways so that we could pose together. 'You look like you're about to keel over.'

She raised her voice again. 'And if anyone else here would like to contribute a donation, however small, I'm sure that the girls would appreciate it.'

'Ah, Miss Mahal . . .' Mr Grimwade, looking completely discombobulated, moved to our side. He held a couple of photos in his hand. 'Thank you for coming. Do you mind?' He held out his hand for the microphone and then addressed the crowd.

'It has just been brought to my attention that last night, despite our stringent security measures, *all* of the contestants managed to break out of the school.' Mr Grimwade glared down at the crowd and I saw George Botley grinning up at me. 'I have the proof here.' And he held up the photos. 'I believe that one of our local businessmen has offered a reward of one thousand pounds?'

'Me!' Mr Gill was bowling his way through the crowd at great speed, staring adoringly up at Molly Mahal. 'It was me!'

Mr Grimwade handed Mr Gill the photos as he bounced onto the stage, but he was too enraptured by Molly to even look at them.

'Oh, well, now, I'm sure a lovely kind man like you could offer the girls just a teeny-weeny bit more,' Molly suggested, grabbing the mike from Mr Grimwade again and fluttering her outsized eyelashes. 'Especially as not one but *all* of the contestants managed to escape.'

'Two thousand pounds!' Mr Gill declared, puffing out his chest expansively.

'Thanks!' I gasped, but my voice was lost in the general celebration.

'And now I must be going,' Molly announced. 'It was wonderful to see you all again.'

She gave everyone on the stage a quick smile and a wave, and then her minders were helping her down from the stage. They whisked her through the playground, stopping only to sign a few more autographs, and then she was inside the limo.

I glanced at my watch as the car moved away. Molly Mahal had been there for just eight minutes, in total. But what a difference she'd made. Mr Grimwade was now directing a group of sixth-formers, including Gareth and Soo-Lin, who were moving through the crowd collecting donations in plastic buckets. I could hear the sweet sound of coins clinking and, even more promisingly, the rustle of notes, over and over and over again.

'I can't believe Molly came!' Jazz kept saying over and over again. 'She's *huge* after *Who's in the House?!*'

'It was very good of her,' Auntie agreed. 'But don't forget it's publicity for her too.'

'Yes, *great* publicity as well,' Geena added. 'I can see the headlines now. *Superstar Molly makes time to visit old friends.* That kind of thing.'

I smiled. 'I don't care,' I said.

And really, I didn't. Molly Mahal's life was all about getting in the newspapers and celebrity magazines, and being on TV, and I didn't mind if she'd only come to Coppergate today because it made her look good to her adoring public. Thanks to her, we'd made a whole heap more money than we would have done otherwise.

And for that I was grateful.

'I have been privileged to hold several naming ceremonies at Coppergate since the school was built.' Mr Morgan looked round at the small but select audience standing in the corridor outside the library doors. 'But I have to say that this one gives me more pleasure than any of them. I would now like to invite Geena, Ambajit and Jasvinder Dhillon to unveil the new name of our library.'

My knees were trembling slightly as I stepped forward. I'd been waiting for this moment for the last six weeks. Christmas had come and gone, and so had the New Year. We'd had a brilliant time, as always, but this was what we had been looking forward to, ever since the end of term.

'Don't cry, Dad,' Jazz warned, joining me and Geena at the doors. A small red velvet curtain was lightly tacked up there, covering the precious plaque.

'Auntie's already got her hanky out,' Geena whispered.

'When you're ready, girls,' said Mr Morgan.

I glanced round at the assembled crowd. Uncle Jai, Baby, Kim, Rocky and Mr Hernandez were there, as well as some of the other teachers and the sixth-formers, including Gareth and Soo-Lin. Mr Gill, Mr Attwal and a few of the other local business people who'd donated money were there too. A photographer from the local newspaper was hovering, preparing to take our picture, along with Martha Rigby and her news crew. Oh, and George Botley, by special invite. Ahem. Well, I couldn't leave him out, could I?

'Thank you for coming, everyone,' Geena said. 'We name this library the Anjleen Dhillon Library.'

'Dedicated to the memory of our lovely mum,' Jazz added.

I tugged at the curtain and it came away, revealing the shiny brass plaque. THE ANJLEEN DHILLON LIBRARY was engraved on it.

It was all quite emotional, and Auntie had to hand round tissues.

Mr Morgan flung open the library doors and we all went in. The change was amazing. All the rickety old furniture had gone, and there were modern chrome and beechwood chairs and tables in its place. Some of the bookcases had been replaced too, and there were shelves and shelves of brand-new books. I felt very proud of us. In the end we'd managed to raise nearly twelve thousand pounds, so we'd given the rest to the hospital where Mum was a patient.

'Isn't this amazing?' Jazz sighed with satisfaction as we wandered around the library a little later, taking it all in. We'd been photographed with the plaque and with Dad, and we'd been interviewed by Martha for the local news programme that evening. 'I always knew we'd raise that money somehow.'

'Oh, excuse me,' I said. 'I thought you said it was impossible. "As impossible as England winning the World Cup or climbing Everest in high heels" were your exact words, I do believe.'

'Face it, Jazz.' Geena shrugged. 'Only someone like Amber could have pulled all this off so spectacularly. I mean, getting Molly Mahal to turn up was a masterstroke.'

Jazz grinned. 'I guess so.'

'Thank you,' I said modestly. As predicted, Molly had got loads of good publicity, and everyone thought she was super-fab for making time in her hectic schedule to do a favour for little old me. Well, good for her. I didn't mind a bit.

I glanced around the library. Baby was talking animatedly to the news crew, detailing her dreams of Bollywood stardom. I don't think they were filming her or even listening, but that didn't stop Baby. Gareth was pretending to talk to Soo-Lin but kept glancing at Geena every so often. George was telling Mr Grimwade in great detail how he'd broken us all out of school on the last night of the contest. Judging by the look on Mr Grimwade's face, he didn't really want to hear it. I wasn't quite sure what I was going to do about George. I obviously owed him a *big* favour for helping us and I was pretty sure that, at some time or another, he would call that favour in. *Help*.

Auntie and Uncle Jai were chatting to Dad. They were fine again, and everything was back to normal. Australia, indeed! I mean, they'd be totally *bored* without us living next door.

'There's one thing we *do* need to talk about though.' I lowered my voice a little. Turning, I checked to see where Kim was but she was over the other side of the library, browsing through some bookshelves. 'We haven't had much time over Christmas.'

'Ooh, you mean Geena and Gareth Parker,' Jazz

said gleefully. 'Yes, we still don't have the full story.'

'There *is* no "full story",' Geena replied. 'I've told you a million times. We went out twice. We split up. But we're going to be friends, just for now.' She glanced down at her fingernails a bit too casually. 'Dad said I can invite him round for tea.'

Jazz and I goggled at her for a second and then we collapsed into hysterical laughter.

'He won't come,' Jazz predicted confidently.

'We'll see,' Geena said.

'Just tell us if he was a good kisser,' Jazz pleaded.

'That's for me to know and you to find out,' Geena retorted with an annoying smile.

'Anyway, I didn't mean Geena and Gareth,' I said quickly as Jazz prepared to argue further. We'd had this conversation so many times over the last six weeks. 'I was talking about Dad. And his mystery lady friend.'

'I didn't think we have anything to worry about there,' said Geena. 'After all, he's never mentioned her since, and he hasn't been working late either. I just thought it had all fizzled out.'

'Maybe she *was* just a friend,' Jazz pointed out. 'Or maybe she was keener on Dad than he was on her.'

I shrugged. 'Maybe. But this might just be the start. There might be others in the future.'

'Others?' Geena raised her eyebrows. 'You're making Dad sound like Casanova.'

'All right,' I said impatiently. 'There might be *someone* else. One woman. Someone special. Someone he wants to marry. Who then, may I remind you, becomes our stepmother.'

Jazz shuddered. 'What a horrible thought.'

'Exactly,' I agreed. 'So there's only one thing for it.'

'And what's that?' asked Geena.

'Well, it's obvious, isn't it?' I replied. 'If Dad is going to get married again, it has to be to someone *we* like. After all,' I went on with a smile, 'we got Auntie and Uncle Jai together, didn't we? So now we need to start looking around for a suitable girlfriend for Dad . . .'

ALSO BY NARINDER DHAMI

BINDI BABES
Meet Amber, Jazz and Geena!

BOLLYWOOD BABES
Join the Babes as they meet a
real Bollywood star!

BHANGRA BABES
Which Babe will win the heart of
the new boy in school?

SUNITA'S SECRET
Can Sunita keep her family secret
at her new school?

DANI'S DIARY
Friendship, family and mysteries
from the past . . .